Bob Freeman

Sea Tramps

A novel by Robert H. Freeman

SHELLBACK PRESS

First Edition

Other books by the same writer -

Requiem for a Fleet
The U.S. Navy at Guadalcanal

Carriers & Cruisers of World War II
Histories of 112 noted American ships.

Troop Transports & Cargo Ships of World War II
Histories of 120 noted American ships.

Copyright (c) 1986 by Robert H. Freeman

Shellback Press
PO Box 2442, Ventnor, N.J., 08406

ISBN: 0-931099-01-3

Manufactured in the U.S.A.

The Log

This book was written in response to the following:

"The LCT had but one commissioned officer and 13 men aboard when they arrived in the South Pacific. The LCTs were not commissioned ships of the Navy, the one officer being designated the Officer-in-Charge. They had insufficient personnel to keeps a ship's log, much less a war diary, and by and large they passed in and out of their service in the Navy leaving no individual record, **except in the memories of those who served in them** or had some service performed by them. Presumably, the LCT Flotilla and Group Commanders kept a log and a war diary, but if they did so, by and large they have not survived to reach normal repositories of such documents."

- Adm. George C. Dyer

"If there was one group of Reserve Officers for whom I had the greatest admiration and sympathy, it was the young LCT officers. Usually, they were the only officer aboard and as such were responsible for the safety of the craft, and also for the harder job of maintaining discipline among the small crew, many of whom were often older than themselves." - Admiral Daniel Barbey.

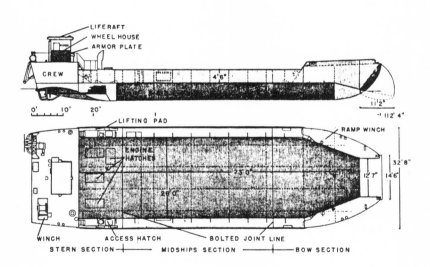

"In New Guinea the LCT operated in a manner for which it was not designed and of which few could have believed it capable.   Living quarters for the crew of two officers and ten men were small, box like compartments intended to house them only during short-haul operations such as crossing the English Channel. But in the Southwest Pacific these craft had to operate continuously in all sorts of tasks ranging from assault echelon to harbor lighterage, and to house their crews for months on end."

- Admiral S.E.Morison

Author's Note -

This book is a work of fiction based on fact. During and after World War Two I served on a variety of landing craft. Because there were so many ships with so many numbers, there may actually have been landing craft with the numbers that I have used in this book, but I had no one vessel in mind when I wrote this novel. All of the characters and ships are a mixture of memory and imagination which can only be called fiction. (With the exception of Chapter 8.)

- R.H.F.

Part I

October 1944

Being an account of the part played by a group of small landing craft in the invasion of the Philippine Islands; and, an investigation into the alleged un-military conduct of the men assigned to serve aboard the LCTs of MacArthur's Navy.

Chapter I

"Welcome Aboard"

LCT-166, Hollandia, New Guinea, October 1944

Ensign Brower was 23 years old in 1944. He was a tall, thin native of Seattle, Washington. He had enlisted in the Navy upon graduating from college in 1943. The Navy promptly sent him to Officer Candidates' School, commissioned him an ensign, and shipped him to the SouthWest Pacific. That was a mistake, because Brower's red hair and fair skin made it impossible for him to acclimate himself to the tropical-equatorial sun that was to be his daily tormentor. Yet this very tormentor was to prove to be the source of his eventual relief.

October of 1944 found Ensign Brower stoically awaiting the arrival of his replacement. All of the men on LCT 166 were stoically awaiting the arrival of their replacements, but Brower actually had one coming. This happy turn of events was the result of his being afflicted with "jungle rot." It was easy to get the rot in the South Pacific where every scratch and cut became infected regardless of how careful one was. Brower was prone to sunburn, blisters, and peeling, so he developed a raging case of the rot. The only cure for such a condition in those days was a transfer to a more salubrious climate.

2 Sea Tramps

So Brower waited, and drank, and slept in his tormented skin. He hardly ever wore anything except a pair of khaki shorts because anything more than that aggravated his condition.

It wasn't Brower's fault that his skin was pro-rot. He wasn't trying to get out of anything. He had skippered the 166 through six landings on as many hostile beaches. He had even been awarded a Purple Heart for being wounded one day while sitting in the officers' "head." Some fragments from a near-miss had penetrated the rusty side of the 166 and had hit him in the ass. After that he was knicknamed "Purple Ass." But the men liked him. He left them alone most of the time. They were very apprehensive about his replacement.

One morning during the first week of October 1944, the long arm of the Navy Bureau of Personnel reached out and deposited one Ensign Lawrence Smyth on the tank deck of the USS Motley (LCT-166). Ensign Smyth might best be described as being "clean cut." He was tall, blond, clear-skinned, and in his early twenties. He was wearing regulation shoes, white socks, khaki trousers, twill belt with shiny buckle, khaki shirt over a T-shirt, and a khaki overseas cap. He was carrying a duffle bag in one hand, a large manila envelope in the other, and a look of incredulity on his face.

It was after 0800 and no one was stirring aboard what was to be his first command. There was not a soul in sight except for someone asleep in a beach chair on the flying bridge. The only sound came from a gasping gasoline generator. The only other sign of life was a wisp of smoke from out the galley stove-pipe. Ensign Smyth was non-plussed. O.C.S. had not prepared him for <u>this</u> type of reception. He tentatively approached the single hatch which offered the only access to the crews' quarters.

His approach was tentative because there were several clothes lines rigged athwart the tank deck which effectively barred his access to the hatch. These lines were three feet above the deck. They were laden with dry laundry. The ensign's problem was how to traverse the obstacles before him without losing his dignity. He had the options of crawling under the lines, or of climbing over them, or of hurdling them (he had been a hurdler on his college track team), or he could cut them. He decided to climb over each one as he pressed down on them in turn. However, he had not anticipated the presence of several laundry pails that had been scattered about the deck as booby-traps to foil clothes thieves in the night. One of these pails was full of soapy water. This was the one into which he stepped. So there, for a moment, stood the new ensign - straddling a clothes line - with one foot in a pail of water.

Down went the ensign; down went the clothes line; down went the clothes - all into one big soapy mess. Ensign Smyth just sat there, for a moment, stunned. He himself had not made a sound for fear that someone might hear him and thus see the predicament that he was in. He did not want his initial impression on the crew to be of <u>this</u> nature.   He silently but furiously dis-entangled himself, rose to his feet, adjusted his uniform, and tried to re-assume his air of command.   No one had witnessed his embarrassment. His dignity may have been wet, but it had not been compromised too badly.   He continued on his original course toward the hatch. The remaining clothes lines and pails did not embarrass him.   He reached the hatch.   He managed to step through it without tripping over the threshold.

To his left he saw someone asleep with his head resting upon his crossed arms upon the mess table. Everyone else was also asleep in their bunks. Had the crew been struck by a mysterious Melanesian malady? thought the   ensign.   He approached the sleeping form   at the table.   He gave it a tentative shake. It grunted.   The ensign shook it again.   An eye opened.   Who the hell is this wet sonofabitch? thought the cook to himself. "Yeah?" he mumbled.

"It's after 0800 and apparently you are the only one awake on this vessel!"

"So?"

"There's even someone asleep on the bridge!"

"Yeah, that's Essex. He had the watch."

"Is it customary to sleep while on watch on this ship?"

"Only when in port."

"What time is reveille around here? I noticed that the flag is up. How can you have Colors without having reveille first?"

"Colors!" yawped the cook. "That flag ain't moved in a year that I know of."

"Do you mean to sit there and tell me that you don't have reveille or Colors aboard this vessel?"

"Not that I know of," confessed the cook.

"Where's Ensign Brower?"

"In his sack. "

"Where's that?"

"You passed it on the way in."

"Where?"

"Over there behind that blanket that's strung up. If youd'a taken another step when you came in youd'a been in his cabin. I'll go roust him for ya if you'd like."

"No, that's all right. Let him sleep. I understand that he's sick."

"Nah, he ain't sick. All he's gots a touch of leprosy."

"Leprosy! What is this, a leper colony? Is that why everyone's asleep? My God, I've been assigned to a plague ship!"

"You been assigned to this ship?"

"Yes, I'm Ensign Brower's replacement."

"Well, that's diff'rent," said the cook as he extended his hand. "My name's Clay, Clay Evers, I'm the cook."

"My name's Smyth, Ensign Smyth, spelled with a 'y'."

"What is?'

"My name, my last name, it's spelled with a 'y'."

"Well ain't that a coincidence, so's my first name."

"Yes, well, does Ensign Brower really have what you said he has?"

"Nah, he just looks like he's got it , but he don't really. Nothin' to be afeared of. We just tell that to strangers to get rid of them when they's nosey. It most always works."

"I'm not surprised," said the relieved replacement as he sat down with his back to the mess table.

"Well, now that that's settled I have but one more question."

"Yes, sir?"

"What's for breakfast?"

"Now you're talkin'. I don't get much call for breakfast 'round here. Too bad, 'cause it's the best meal of the day."

"What's on the menu?"

"Bacon, scrambled eggs, home fries, coffee, and toast."

"Sounds great," replied the ravenous ensign.

"Yeah. The only thing wrong with it is that the bacon comes out of a can, and the eggs and spuds is dehydrated. But the coffee and bread is real!"

"Well even so, it still sounds great. How come no one gets up to eat?"

"Oh I guess they're tired of the same thing everyday. Or else they're hung over and don't feel like eatin'. Or they just like sleepin' in the cool of the morning. I don't know why I even bother to get up. Habit, I guess. But every now and then somebody gets hungry. Essex, for example. He usually likes to eat when he comes off watch."

"You mean that body up there in the beach chair?"

"Yeah, that's Essex. He's our signalman."

"Is he rated?"

"Sure, he's a first-class signalman."

"Hasn't he ever been busted for sleeping on watch?"

"Busted? No one ever gets busted in <u>this</u> outfit!"

"Why not?"

"Because the whole fuckin' outfit's busted, if you know what I mean," said the cook giving the ensign a knowledgeable look.

"No, I don't know what you mean."

"Well you will, Mister Smyth, you will." Who does this guy think he is? thought the cook to himself as he put some bacon in the frying pan. Him comin' in here talkin' about Colors and reveille and bustin' people. He'll be lucky if I don't bust him with this here fryin' pan!

Clay Evers seldom lost his temper. He was an easy-going southerner who was in his third "hitch" in the Navy. He was about thirty years old, but he looked older because of his sallow skin and watery eyes which were traceable to his fondness for strong spirits. His pale skin was an anomaly among the men of the 166 who were all SOUWESPAC brown. Clay never went out in the sun if he could avoid it. He preferred to sleep away the days and drink away the nights with brief interruptions for cooking.

Clay kept his unkempt hair short by cutting it himself about once a week. He shaved about as often. Thus he gave the impression that he was preparing himself to play the lead in a USO production of **The Drunkard**. Clay would never have passed inspection in the real Navy, but the 166 was glad to have him. Good cooks were hard to come by.

Ensign Smyth decided that the best course of action at that moment was not to ask any more questions. So he just sat there with his back to the long , narrow mess table. He looked about him.

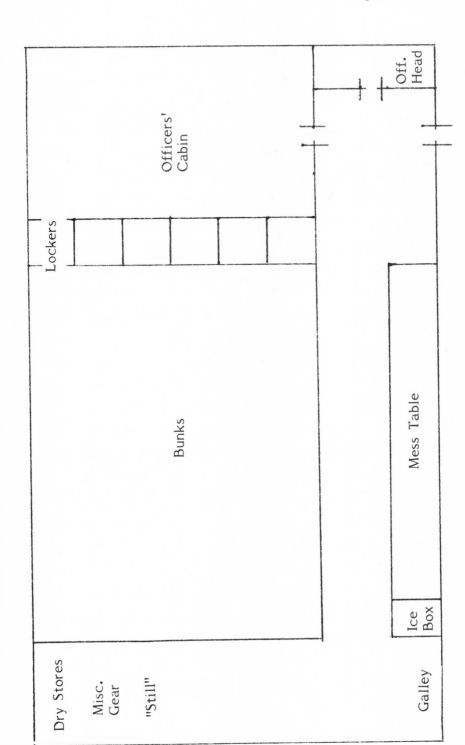

The compartment measured about 12 by 30 feet.

Into that space were crammed the officer's quarters, bunks and lockers for ten men, the galley, the mess table, a refrigerator (domestic model), and a storage area for dry stores. Three port holes had been cut in the steel transom to provide some light and less ventilation. The only other source of natural light and fresh air was the hatch previously mentioned. The only source of artificial light was a single bulb above the mess table.

It was no wonder that the men liked to sleep-in during the coolness of the morning. A steel hull absorbs heat all day long and then gives it back all night long. But there were a few hours in the early morning when there was a merciful balance of convection currents that made life briefly bearable within that steel box. Insulation and air-conditioning were undreamed of in the amphibious navy of 1944. Even a fan was a luxury. They once had a fan on the 166, but it wore out.

"Good morning, Clay," said signalman Essex as he stepped through the hatch. His uniform consisted of a pair of khaki shorts and a GI blanket which hung from his shoulders. Essex was a tall, thin 19-year old from Upstate New York. His long, dark hair, dark eyes, aquiline nose, brown skin, and GI blanket combined to give him the look of the last of the Mohawks.

"Mornin', Tom" replied the cook. "Have a good sleep?"

"Pretty good. The generator only stopped once."

"Good. Want some breakfast?"

"Right. That's what woke me up. I smelled that bacon fryin'. Who's this?" he asked as he looked at the wet, dumbstruck ensign.

"Oh, this here's Brower's replacement. Ensign Smyth meet Tom Essex." They shook hands. "Glad to meetcha, sir. Yeah, you look like a replacement all right. I ain't seen a wet regulation uniform since the day Brower got his medal in the rain."

"Ensign Brower's been decorated?" asked the incredulous Smyth.

"Sure," replied Essex, "the Purple Heart."

"He was wounded?"

"Only in the ass," said Brower as he stepped out from behind the blanket, "but people _do_ get hit on these barges. Life isn't all fun and games in the amphibs, even though that may be your first impression." Brower was wearing the white bathrobe that he had borrowed from the hospital ship. "I'm George Brower," he said as he extended his hand. "I'm sure glad to see _you_."

Smyth stood at attention, saluted, and said, "Ensign Larry Smyth reporting for duty, _sir_." He handed his large manila envelope to Brower.

"Yes, well, at ease Mister Smyth, and welcome aboard."   Brower turned to the cook and said, "A cuppa coffee for your new C.O., Cookie, and one for me,too."   The cook happily complied with his request. He also poured one for Essex and one for himself.

"Yes, Larry," said Brower as he stirred the sugar and canned milk in his cup, "we don't spend all of our time in dandy rear areas like Hollandia. Now and then we pay a visit on the Nips.   Don't we ,Cookie?"

"Yeah, 'bout once a month."

"Once a month!"   exclaimed Smyth.

"Sometimes more."

"We've been pretty busy lately," said Essex. "But for some reason our group wasn't invited to the beach party at Moratai last month."

"Every time that MacArthur moves through these islands or along this coast it's the amphibs that take him where he wants to go," said Brower. "It's not the PT-boats that land the army and marines here, we do it.   So welcome aboard if you want to see some action, but don't expect any recognition."

"PT-boats for Chris' sake," spat Essex. "They ain't done nothin' but chase Jap barges since we pulled out of the Solomons. We've been bustin' our ass since since then, but who ever heard of us?"

"The Navy don't admit we exist," said the cook.

"We embarrass them," said Brower.

"And the army hates out guts."

"Even the marines hate us."

"They hate everybody."

"We don't even get paid," added the cook.

"Oh shut the fuck up," yelled the bosun from his rack. "You never had it so good, ya goddam bean burner. What's for breakfast?"

"What is it with you?" responded the cook. "You always ask the same question, and you always get the same answer."

"I can't help it. I'm still dreamin' when I wake up. I'm dreamin' of fresh eggs, and butter, and grapefruit, and all them good things. But anyway, put some on for me, whatever it is." He rolled over on his stomach and asked, "Hey, what are all you guys doin' up so early?" He rolled out of his rack and asked, "Who's this?" as he pointed at Smyth.

"This is your new C.O., Ensign Smyth," replied the happy Brower. "We're havin' a 'welcome aboard' party."

"No shit?" responded the awed bosun. "He actually showed up?"

"I shit you not."

"Well, what are all these guys still doin' in the sack? Hit the deck!" roared the bosun as he went around to each rack to push each inert form. Soon the remainder of the crew had rolled out to stand in sleepy confusion before the other half of the crew.

"Wake up, stand up, this here is your new C.O."
The men didn't know what to do in response to this
startling news, so they just stood there.

"Thank you, 'Boats'," said Brower.   "I want to
introduce you men to Ensign Smyth here who, as the
bosun has already pointed out, is to be your new C.O.
as soon as I can get my heroic sore ass off this here
barge."

Brower went through the ranks introducing Smyth
to Motor Machinist Mate Berger, Seaman Frisch,
Fireman Temple, Seaman Mack, Gunner's Mate Zale,
Seaman Dugan, and Seaman Pacelli. That was the
whole crew - five petty officers, four seamen, and
one fireman. And, oh yes, one ensign.

The cook yelled for his helper - Seaman Pacelli -
to turn-to. He was about to have the biggest call for
a reconstituted breakfast that he had ever had during
his tenure as cook aboard the 166.   It was a
memorable moment and an auspicious introduction for
Ensign Smyth.   He decided that life aboard an LCT
might not be so bad after all.   As in any other ship,
it all depended on the crew. And the crew of the 166
was as agreeable a collection of young Americans as
could be found aboard any vessel in the U.S. Navy,
including PT-boats.

Following breakfast, Brower took his replacement on a tour of the ship. Their first stop was the "captain's cabin." This space was just large enough for a set of bunks, two lockers, a small table, and a folding chair. It was partitioned off from the crews' quarters by a row of lockers.

"Double bunks?" remarked Smyth.

"Yeah, can you believe it? One officer is too many. The bosun runs the ship. The men know what to do. They really don't need us."

"Then why?"

"I don't know. The Navy must have a lot of junior Reserve Officers that it doesn't know what to do with. Why else?"

"Indeed, why else?"

"Cheer up. Look at this," said Brower as he opened a hatch adjacent to the cabin. "Your own private 'head'. What more could you want?"

"Does it work?"

"Oh, you've had some experience with these things?"

"Somewhat."

"Well this one works most of the time; however, it's a bit erratic ever since we got hit," said Brower as he put a hand on his rear end. "Come along, I'll show you the wheel house."

They left the compartment, turned left, and ascended a short ladder to the wheel house deck. Then they stepped inside another steel box. This one measured app. ten feet in length, eight feet in width, and seven feet in heighth. It contained the wheel, the binnacle to which the wheel was secured, and the compass which sat atop the binnacle.   The wheel house did   not show any signs of radar equipment, Loran, or gyro-compass.   It also did not contain any radio equipment.

"Is that compass your only aid to navigation?" asked Smyth in dis-belief.

"That's it."

"And you don't have any radio equipment?"

"That's right."

"Then how do you manage to communicate with anyone?"

"There's a blinker-light on the bridge above us, and Essex is a . . ."

" . . . a first-class signalman. Yes, I know."

"How'd you know that?" asked Brower.

"How do you manage to navigate with nothing more than a compass?"

"We follow the leader."

"It all seems rather tenuous."

"Yes, it is rather tenuous.   This is a Landing Craft Tenous," Brower laughed insanely.   Smyth did not join in.

Once Brower had recovered from his fit he asked, "What did you major in in college?"

"English Lit."

"Oh, that explains it."

"Explains what?"

"The way you talk. You sound like an English novel."

"Oh really? I wouldn't be surprised if it were **Alice in Wonderland**," replied the literate Mister Smyth. "What are those levers for over there?"

"Engine controls. They're Berger's responsibility."

"Who's Berger?"

"The motor-mac."

"Come, I'll show you the main battery."

On either side of the wheel house was located a 20mm anti-aircraft gun enclosed in a canvas shroud. Each gun was provided with a "ready box" containing four circular magazines at the ready.

"Are these our total armament?"

"No, we have an assortment of rifles and tommy guns in case we're ever called upon to help out on the beach."

"You're kidding!"

"No, I'm not kidding."

"And have you ever been called upon to help out on the beach?" asked Ensign Smyth who had suddenly grown very tired.

"Not yet, but others have. When they call for a 'special landing party', that's it."

"You're kidding?"

"No, we can be dragooned at any time. We are truly amphibious.   We even have a pile of helmets, canteens, and webbed belts up forward in the port locker.   There's several cases of thirty caliber ammo up there, too. Come on, I'll show you."

"But what becomes of the ship if the crew is dragooned?"

"It just becomes another derelict on the beach. We are very expendable." (Sixty-seven LCTs were lost during the war to a variety of causes.)

"And how have you managed to avoid such a fate?" asked Smyth with more than just professional interest.

"I make sure to drop the stern anchor when we're about a hundred feet from the beach. Then if things get too hot you can always pull yourself off." Brower pointed out the anchor and its winch before they descended to the tank deck. They began to walk toward the bow.

"This sure is a big bastard. How much can it carry?"

"Didn't they tell you <u>anything</u> about LCTs in OCS?"

"Are you kidding? I didn't even know what an LCT was until a week ago. This outfit is a well-kept secret."

"Yeah, well, one of these big bastards can carry four large tanks,or four large trucks, or 180 tons of supplies, or 300 infantrymen standing up, or fifty infantrymen lying down."

"Lying down?"

"On stretchers.   Sometimes we take a load of wounded off the beach. We're very versatile. We're also very sloppy this morning," said Brower as he eyed the rows of clothes lines which barred them from going forward.   He yelled for the bosun to get someone to remove the obstacles.   The ensigns continued their tour after seaman Frisch had cleared the way.

A large locker was located on either side of the ramp.   The one on the port side contained the items that Brower had mentioned plus misc. bosun's gear. The locker on the other side contained more of the same plus the crew's "head."

"Does this one work?" asked Smyth while looking inside the locker.

"Sometimes, but they only use it when we're underway or when the weather is foul. Usually they just hang their ass over the stern. That always get a laugh."

"And what's that oil-drum for up there over the head?"

"That holds the water for our showers. See the shower head sticking out just above the hatch? We got that from a native head-peddler," again Brower laughed insanely.

"Our showers provide another laugh," he said after he had recovered, "especially when we're on the beach with our ramps down," and with that he went into another fit.

This duty is going to be a million laughs, thought an unsmiling Ensign Smyth. "What's that thing over the port locker"

"That's the ramp winch."

"Does it work?"

"Usually."

"It, too, is slightly erratic, I take it?"

"Yeah, like everything on this barge."

"And what about the men, are they erratic, too?"

"Of course. What do you think a year or two of this duty does to a man? It changes you mister, it changes you. Your friend, Shakespeare, would call it a 'sea change'."

"Have you changed?" asked Smyth.

"Of course."

"For better or worse."

"How the hell do I know?" responded Brower angrily. "I won't know until I've gotten away from this. It's all a matter of perspective, isn't it?"

"Yes, I suppose so. By the way, what's your perspective on discipline?"

"What do you mean by that?"

"When I came on board this morning I saw Essex asleep in the beach chair on the bridge. He was supposed to be on watch. Do you ignore that sort of thing?"

"The main reason for having a man on watch while we are in port," said Brower in an effort to control his temper, "is to make sure that our generator does not run out of gas. That is important because that generator is our only source of electricity. If it runs out of gas that means that our refrigerator will defrost and our beer will get warm! If that happened then the men would take care of Essex much better than I could. No, we're not much for 'Rules and Regs' around here. But if an ass has to be kicked, the bosun will do it. He doesn't need any guidance from me."

"Listen," continued Brower, "these guys have enough to put up with without goading them with the **Bluejacket's Manual.** You see the way they have to live. What would you do to discipline them? Take away their 'liberty'? Restrict them to the ship? Don't make me laugh! You'll learn to live and let live in this outfit. You really don't have any alternative unless you're suicidal. Are you suicidal, Mister Smyth?

"No, of course not."

"All right then. Relax and try to enjoy it."

"Hey, Skipper," yelled one of the men on the bridge, "We're gettin' a signal from the '34'." (Their command ship, LCI 34.)

"Okay, give them an Able-Sugar on the light. We'll be right there." Brower ran aft to the compartment followed by Smyth. Brower yelled for Essex and then climbed to the bridge. Smyth and Essex were right behind him. They received the following message: Proceed to Liberty ship **Alex Smithers** to off-load cargo.

"And where the hell might that be?" asked Brower of no one in particular. "There's about a hundred 'Liberties' around here."

"We'll just have to cruise around till we find her, I guess," offered Essex. "Just like we always do."

"Who ever heard of a 'her' named **Alex Smithers**?" asked one of the men.

"Who ever heard of <u>anyone</u> named **Alex Smithers**?" replied another.

"Maybe they mean Alexis Smith?"

"Yeah, let's cruise around till we find <u>her</u>!"

"She ain't here. She moved to San Diego to be near her mother."

"How do you know?"

"I read it in a movie magazine."

"Maybe she'll come back with the USO."

"Maybe you need your head examined."

"Okay," said Brower, "knock off the bullshit. Get the bosun to roust them out. Let's haul ass."

The men did as they were told. The two ensigns remained on the bridge. One wore a slightly wet regulation uniform; the other wore a white bathrobe.

Motor Machinist Mate Second Class Berger and Gunner's Mate Third Class Zale entered the wheel house. Zale would man the wheel while "Motor Mac" Berger manned the engine controls. Berger started the engines. The lines were cast off from the "T" adjacent to them. They slowly moved off.

"Where away?" asked Zale's voice as it emanated from the voice-tube which made communication possible between the wheel house and the bridge located directly above it.

"Try that area off to starboard," yelled Brower into the tube. "I'll try to pick her out with my glasses."

"Okay," replied the disembodied Zale.

"Whose got the wheel?" asked Smyth.

"Zale. He's our best helmsman." GM 3/c Zale had learned how to handle boats back home on the waters which surround and infiltrate the eastern end of Long Island, New York. Zale was 19 years old. He was a little on the short side, stocky, with dark curly hair, blue eyes, and a great smile.

Motor Mac Berger, on the other hand, came from the opposite end of Long Island - Brooklyn. The reason why there is always a "kid from Brooklyn" in every war story about World War II is simply because King's County, N.Y. - Brooklyn - supplied more men to the armed forces than did any other county in the United States.

Berger was a little older than Zale, and a little heavier. He had remarkable strength and endurance to be able to survive the rigors of their small engine room - the Black Hole of Amphibia. But too many hours in too many engine rooms had done something to his head. He had to be watched constantly. He was a dangerous man to drink with.

"Why do we have to off-load a ship?" asked Smyth. "Why doesn't she go to the pier?"

"The pier's all jammed up. You'd have to wait a month to get alongside it. Anyway, off-loading is one of our jobs. This will be good experience for you."

As the 166 slowly cruised the bay, Ensign Smyth became aware of the hundreds of ships assembled there. Not many of them were being off-loaded.

"Why aren't more of the Ts working these ships?" Smyth asked.

"Because most of them are going to be unloaded somewhere else."

"Where?"

"I don't know.   You'll have to ask General MacArthur about that.

Silence.

"Yeah, that's right," said Brower, "and I'm goin' to miss all the fun.   Ain't that a shame!" At that moment he spotted the **Smithers.**   "There she is, Zale, just off to starboard," he yelled in the tube.

"Will you stop yellin' in the goddam tube!" yelled Zale. "I'm goin' deaf down here!"

"Sorry," said Brower in a more moderate voice.

"That's better.   Now what are you tryin' to tell me?"

"I think I see the ship just off to starboard. That pile of rust with the green stack.   Do you see it?"

"Yeah, I think so.   What side to?"

"Put us port to port.   That's the way her booms are rigged."

"Okay, Skipper."

"Boats," yelled the 'skipper' to the bosun down on the tank deck, "port side to."

"Okay," he responded.   "Get them fenders over the port side, " he yelled at his gang.   "We don't wanna scratch our rust, do we?"

"Whose lines are we gonna use, Boats? asked Seaman Dugan.

"Theirs."

"What if they don't give us theirs?"

"Then we'll haul ass and leave 'em here."

The 166 scrunched alongside the **Smithers.**

"Drop us your lines," yelled the bosun up the towering side of the Liberty ship.

"Fuck you," came a voice from above.

"Listen, you prick," yelled the bosun. "It's a helluva lot easier for you to drop us your lines than it is for us to send ours up to you. So stop fuckin'-the-dog and drop your lines or you'll never get out of here!"

That convinced them.   They lowered their three-inch hawsers to the deck of the 166 to be secured around her bitts.   The off-loading began. Cargo nets loaded with wooden crates and cardboard cases began to descend on to the deck.   The sailors then did the work of longshoremen.   However, it would have been difficult to distinguish them from natives.   They were almost as dark as the natives as they climbed over that load in their bare feet, GI shorts, and straw hats.   These semi-natives emptied the cargo nets which were then hoisted aloft to be returned to the ship's hold for another load. But there was something different about that load.

"Jesus, look at this - beer, cigarettes, uniforms! We hit the jackpot!"

The men played it cool until they had finished the job and were safely away from the ship.   Then they went over that load like ants at a picnic.

Every locker and other available space was suddenly crammed with all of the beer and cigarettes that they could hold. A few cases of uniforms were also purloined. Ensign Smyth was horrified.

"Look at them!" he shouted. "They're committing piracy! Do something!"

"Do what?" replied Brower. "I don't see anything." He spoke into the voice tube and said, "Put us alongside the '34'. We'll give Uncle Ben some of these goodies."

"Who's Uncle Ben?" asked the benumbed Ensign Smyth.

"He's our flotilla commander - Lieutenant Benjamin Bell. He likes goodies, too."

"But this is <u>stealing</u>! You're going to give him stolen property - stolen <u>government</u> property! We'll all go to the brig for life!"

"No we won't. This isn't stealing. It might be considered stealing if we got paid, too, but we don't get paid; therefore, this is not stealing," rationalized Ensign Brower. "Since they don't give us any money to buy these things with, then we have to get them some other way. I like to think of this as 'foraging'."

"You never get paid?"

"Hardly ever. Oh it doesn't matter. What would we do with money? There's no women or liquor over here. If we had money we'd just piss it away on beer and cards.

This way we get free beer and no hard feelings. The money stays on the books and we collect it all when we get home.   A hundred and fifty bucks a month. That adds up after a few years!"

They pulled alongside LCI 34 to drop off a few cases of "goodies."   Then they headed for the beach. They slid up as far as they could go on the wet sand, dropped the ramp, and secured from their sea details.   Army trucks were waiting for them.   They backed over the ramp as soon as it was down. Several soldiers came aboard to load the trucks under the watchful eyes of two MPs.   The crew of the   166   watched   their   efforts   with   vigilant dis-interest.   It took the army the remainder of the day to unload the 166.   Along about sunset a colonel, two other officers, and the same two MPs came storming aboard.

"Where's my scotch?" yelled the colonel. "You bastards   took my scotch and I want it back!"

The   crew   of   the   166   went   forward   to   repel boarders.

"What scotch?" asked Brower in all innocence.

"There   was   supposed   to   be   a case of scotch in that load!   My case of scotch, and it's not here! You've got it!   Give it to me or by God we'll take it back!"

"We don't have your goddam scotch,"   protested Brower.   "Do we?" he asked as he turned to face his crew.

He was drowned in protestations of innocence. "There," he said as he turned back to the colonel. "We don't have it. Those 'feather merchants' on the ship must have taken it." The crew agreed with that.

"Oh yeah?" fumed the colonel. "Well I think it's on this ship, and we're gonna search it just to be sure!"

"Oh no you're not!" said Brower as his crew lined up from port to starboard.

"And who the hell are you?" yelled the colonel at the man in the white bathrobe.

"I am Ensign Brower. I am in command of this vessel on which you are trespassing! You do not have any jurisdiction on this or any other naval vessel! The only way that you can get to us is through our flotilla commander - Lieutenant Benjamin Bell - who is presently on LCI number 34 out there somewhere on the bay. However, he may be at the Officers' Club this evening at which time you may have a chat with him."

"What's your name again?" demanded the red-faced colonel.

"Brower. Ensign George Brower, USNR."

"Write that down, Sergeant," said the colonel to the MP standing next to him. "And write down the number of this so-called ship. And the next time that any one of these goddam sea tramps gets in trouble - in my jurisdiction - I'm gonna see to it personally that he gets twenty fucking years in the stockade! IS THAT CLEAR?"

Silence. The colonel and his party departed. It was Brower's finest hour. It was also his time to go. He returned to his cabin to dig out his khaki uniform. It did not take hin very long to change his clothes and to pack his few possessions in a moldy suitcase. He was a thing of splendor when he emerged from his cabin to a chorus of whistles.

"Hey, Skipper, where's your campaign ribbons? They won't know you're a hero without 'em."

"Yeah, and where's your Purple Heart?"

"Are you gonna tell 'em how you got it?"

"Sure I'm gonna tell 'em," said Brower easily slipping into their patois. "I'm gonna be the biggest fuckin' hero on the West Coast. But everytime I look out over this big fuckin' ocean I'm gonna think of you guys. And I want you to remember me. And I want you to be good to Ensign Smyth here. He's new at this racket and he's gonna need a lot of help. I'm gonna be writin' to him, and he's gonna be writin' to me. So if I hear that you're fuckin'-up more than usual I'm gonna write to that colonel and tell him that you drank his scotch. So you better do for Ensign Smyth like you did for me. Okay?"

"Okay," they all responded.

"Now I'm supposed to sign your orders or somethin', ain't I?" mumbled Brower. He returned to his cabin to look for Smyth's manila envelope. He re-emerged to sit at the mess table to open it. The men surrounded him.   He found Smyth's orders and signed them.   His orders were also in there.   He removed them and then he noticed a third sheet of paper.   That one announced his promotion to the rank of Lieutenant (jg). There was a pair of new silver bars at the bottom of the envelope. The crew went wild when he announced his promotion.   He replaced his dull gold bars with his new silver ones. He was happy for the first time in a long time. He said goodbye to his friends, and then he and Smyth were off to the Officers' Club   together. That was the last time that the crewmen of the 166 saw their ex-skipper. They stayed on the beach that night, but none of them dared go ashore for fear of running into the colonel. And what the hell, who needed to go ashore? They had all of the beer and scotch that they needed right there on the 166. It turned out to be a most memorable evening.   Not enchanted, but memorable.

"Life was particularly rugged on the small craft - the LCTs, and APCs, and SCs - but they enjoyed a freedom from regulations and etiquette of the naval service not enjoyed by larger ships."

- Admiral Barbey.

Chapter 2

Portents

Even a Kookaburra bird flying high over Humboldt Bay would have noticed the increase in shipping activity below. General MacArthur was once again assembling his amphibious navy for another leap northward. Only this time it was going to be the big leap - His Return to the Philippines.

That particular Kookaburra bird, however, was not interested in history. It was looking for a large group of LCTs on which to light. It preferred LCTs because the crew members of those craft were not hostile to birds whose raucous laughter was apt to offend the crew members of more stately vessels. But the crew of an LCT could relate to such a bizarre bird, for they too were odd birds in the eyes of the U.S. Navy.

"What the hell is that goddam riot all about?" yelled Ensign Smyth from his rack to no one in particular.

"It's that Kookaburra bird," replied the cook's voice from beyond the lockers. "It's back again."

"Well go out and shoot the goddam thing, whatever it is. I've never heard such an outrageous noise in all my life."

Smyth slowly sat up on the edge of his rack. His powers of comprehension were somewhat under a cloud that morning.   He looked about him for a cigarette. "What time, is it?" he yelled.

"Ten o'clock in the morning," replied the cook.

"You got any coffee out there?"

"Plenty," answered the cook.

"Good. Pour me a cup. I'm comin' out."

The Ensign Smyth that emerged from his cabin was in sharp contrast to the one that had appeared app. 24 hours earlier.   His uniform would not have passed inspection that morning. And a malevolent black eye gave a satanic cast to his clean-cut features.

"What happened to you?" exclaimed the cook as he admired his C.O.'s shiner.

"Brower and Uncle Ben and me took on Colonel Scotch and his goons in the club last night.   It was beautiful, but thank God that there was more Navy than Army there or we'd all be in his stockade right now - for twenty fuckin' years!   I don't know how I got back here.   Are we still on the beach?"

"Yeah."

"Well we gotta get off before the colonel shows up again with more of his bully-boys.   Boats," he yelled at a sleeping form as he shook it. "Boats, wake up, we gotta get outta here before the colonel shows up! Wake up!"

"What?" moaned the bosun. "Are you nuts or somethin'?"

"Come on, get up. We gotta get off the beach before it's too late. The tide's just right," he guessed. "If we don't get off right now we won't get off at all, and I'll end up in the stockade!"

"All right, all right. Ya know, <u>you</u> weren't the <u>only</u> one drinkin' last night."

"Never mind that, we have to get off this beach right now or else!"

"Or else what?"

"Or else we'll be . . . dragooned!"

"What?"

"Dragooned," continued the inspired ensign, "that's the worst kind of punishment!"

"Yeah, it sounds like it," said the bosun as he rolled out of his rack. "All right, you guys," he shouted, "drop your cocks and grab your socks. We gotta get off this beach before we get marooned or somethin'. Come on, shake a leg, hit the deck, get your ass up."

The men grudgingly responded to these entreaties. Fireman Temple staggered forward to start the ramp winch. It coughed and caught on the second pull of of the lanyard.   The ramp came up slowly on Smyth's forecastle. He was safe behind his ramparts. Luckily the tide <u>was</u> high, and the 166 was able to elude the colonel's grasp.

"Where away?" yelled Zale from within the wheel house.

"Wait a goddam minute!" yelled the skipper as he climbed to the bridge. "Okay," he said once he had achieved the commanding height, "take us to our anchorage. We do have an anchorage don't we?"

"Yes sir, to the anchorage."

Ensign Smyth breathed a sigh of relief.

"What side to, Skipper?" asked the bosun from the tank deck.

"Starboard side to," guessed the new skipper of the old 166. "Is that okay?" he whispered into the voice tube.

"Okay," came the reply.

"Standby for a starboard approach," yelled the bosun to his gang. "Get them fenders over, and get them   lines ready or I'll have your liver for breakfast!" His sluggish deck gang suddenly came alive.

Shortly they were back in the safety of the anchorage with the rest of the flotilla. The bosun decided to wake everybody up by lowering the ramp to water level so that they could go swimming in the emerald water of Humboldt Bay. All but the cook, that is.   He was busily preparing another huge breakfast

The men were soon clambering back aboard. They did not like to loll in those infested waters. A dip, followed by a fast shower, was enough to blow away the fumes and to put an edge on their appetites.   After they had eaten their fill they just lounged around enjoying the view.

Humboldt Bay is one of the world's great natural harbors.   It offers as magnificent a marine vista as any to be seen anywhere in the world.   Yet few ever saw it after October of 1944 because it is cursed by its remoteness, diseases, and weather.

Geographically it is located but two degrees south of the equator.   Exotic diseases are endemic there. The monsoon brings months of humidity, rain, and clouds.   But oh, the clouds!   At times they rise tier upon tier in great tumbling masses all the way to glory.   Each tier may be a different color - amber, saffron, violet, rose, white - and all against a background of Delft blue.   Such a sight as to convince a man that he would not want to be anywhere else in the world at that moment.

Lieutenant Benjamin Bell was enjoying the view from the bridge of his LCI when he received an order to report to Vice Admiral Daniel Barbey aboard his command ship the **Blue Ridge.**

Admiral "Uncle Dan" Barbey was the commander of the Seventh Amphibious Force (MacArthur's Navy) in the Southwest Pacific. He planned the landing of one million soldiers and marines in 56 amphibious operations against the Japanese. Admiral Barbey was 55 years old in 1944. He was a native of Portland, Oregon. He had graduated from the Naval Academy in 1912. "Uncle Dan" was a brick of a man with a leonine head. MacArthur's victories would not have been possible without the admiral's "amphibs." His men and ships made the leap-frog approach from New Guinea to Leyte and beyond possible. Yet few outside of the Navy would recognize the admiral's name. This is so because MacArthur would not tolerate any other "personality" on his team. Thus he was always in the general's shadow. That was also the way that the admiral wanted it.

Lieutenant Benjamin Bell was one of the admiral's group commanders. He was a 35-year old native of Topeka, Kansas. Lieutenant Bell was a former school teacher turned warrior. He had the sloping shoulders and quizzical gaze inherent in all school masters. He was as thin and as tough as an oak rail. Sixteen amphibious operations against the Japanese had tempered his humanity and sharpened his cynicism. He would never return to the classroom.

The following is a re-creation of a transcript of a conversation between Admiral Barbey and Lieutenant Bell which may have sounded something like this:

BARBEY: We are returning to the Philippines on the twentieth of this month. We want your group to join us there.

BELL: Sir?

BARBEY: Didn't you hear me, Ben? We are returning to the Philippines on the twentieth, and we want your group to join us there.

BELL: Oh yes,sir, and we would like to join you there, sir, but how are we supposed to get there?

BARBEY: Don't be flip with me, Ben. I don't have much left in the line of patience.

BELL: Excuse me, sir. I didn't mean to be flip. You said that you wanted my group to join you in the Philippines?

BARBEY: Yes, that's right.

BELL: Where, sir?

BARBEY: Where what? Are you all right, Ben?

BELL: Where in the Philippines, sir?

BARBEY: Leyte Gulf.

BELL: And how far is that from here, sir?

BARBEY: Twelve hundred miles.

BELL: Jesus! You know as well as I that LCTs were not made for that kind of duty. They'll never make it that far!

BARBEY: I know they weren't made for that kind of duty, but that's the kind of duty they've had, isn't it?
BELL: Yes, sir.
BARBEY: And that's the kind of duty they've done, isn't it?
BELL: Yes, sir.
BARBEY: So why can't they do it again?
BELL: Because they're worn out! There's been twenty landings in the past sixteen months.
BARBEY: I know that only too well!
BELL: The men are punchy; discipline is shot to hell; half of them are "asiatic", and now they're expected to sail those broken-down barges to the Philippines! It can't be done!
BARBEY: It can be done and it will be done! The General wants to share the honor of liberating the Philippines with all of his men. And he will be unhappy unless all of his ships, and planes, and men are there. Is that clear?
BELL: Yes, sir. That is very clear. And my men and I will be delighted to share the honor with the General.
BARBEY: That's more like it.
BELL: What's your plan for getting us there?
BARBEY: Your fifty LCTs will be escorted by twenty-five LCIs and an LST repair ship. Draw all the rations that you need at our supply depot. You will stop-over at Biak to replenish your fuel and water.

BELL: There's 900 miles of open water between Biak and Leyte. Do you really think that a motley fleet of landing craft can make a trip like that?

BARBEY: They went from Aitape to Morotai last month, and that's more than 900 miles!

BELL: Yes, but they were in sight of land for most of that distance, and they were escorted by the big boys. We won't have those comforts once we leave Biak!

BARBEY: Damn it, Ben. If we didn't think you could do it we wouldn't ask you to go. We have never told you to damn the torpedoes and the casualties. That's not our style.

BELL: Yes sir, I know.

BARBEY: We have the lowest casualty rate of any combat outfit in the world. We only lost 150 men when we took this place. The General hasn't taken any heavy losses since Buna, and that was long before this outfit was even born. So stop worrying. You will get there!

BELL: Yes, sir. Will we be travelling light or heavy?

BARBEY: Light.

BELL: Then we won't be in the invasion itself?

BARBEY: No, I don't want you there until the 25th. The area should be secured by then. If you maintain an average speed of four knots you will be able to cover the distance in twelve days; thirteen, with a stop-over at Biak.

BELL: If the weather is good, and if we don't run into
any Japs.

BARBEY: The Japs are going to be too busy to bother
with your motley group, as you call them.

BELL: What about breakdowns?

BARBEY: That's what the repair ship is for. And if
necessary, each LCI can tow one LCT. Surely not
more than half of your Ts will require that!

BELL: Let's hope not. When do we leave?

BARBEY: On the morning of the 13th, right after
the main convoy has left.

BELL: What about charts?

BARBEY: You will receive your orders and your
chart first thing in the morning. Any more questions?

BELL: No sir, not at the moment.

BARBEY: Good. Well, goodbye, Ben. Good luck. I'll
see you and your men and your ships in Leyte Gulf
on the 25th. The General and I are depending on you.
We will need your group in the difficult months ahead.
Get them there! And, oh yes, Ben, there may be a
promotion in it for you.

BELL: Thank you, sir. We will do our best. Goodbye.

BARBEY: Goodbye, Ben, and good sailing.

A promotion! he thought to himself as he descended the gangway.   There's going to be more than a goddam promotion in this before it's over. God help me.   God help us all!   He boarded the waiting LCVP, jumped into its well, and told the coxswain to return him to his ship. He was still not totally convinced that his small   ships could make the proposed journey, but he knew that finer minds than his had considered the risks and had found them acceptable.   MacArthur was not the man to be wasteful of his men.   He kept repeating that to himself, and it was a great comfort to him.

"The LCT was a short-range craft, 112 feet long, with a bow ramp, that could carry medium-sized tanks, or their equivalent. Its speed was five or six knots, depending on its load and sea conditions.

"At first there was no provision for crew accommodations, or for storage space for food, water, or spare parts, as these craft were expected to be used only for short runs in the vicinity of shore bases."

- Admiral Barbey

LCT at Kiriwina

First landing of the 7th Amphibious Force - 30 June 1943. Distance from staging area - 710 miles from Townsville, Australia.

Chapter 3

Scuttlebutt

As you know, the landing craft under Lieutenant Bell's command were not radio-equipped for communication between ships or the shore. All messages had to be sent by blinker-light, or hand-flags, or loud-mouth. So in order for him to contact each of his officers he had to send boats carrying a written message saying that they were to meet ashore the next day in the messhall on Pancake Hill, that being the only large building in the area.

Rumor and scuttlebutt and conjecture followed in the wake of each boat as it made its rounds. "What's up?   What's the dope? What's the scoop?" rose in a growing chorus over the flat-bottomed fleet. The officers were non-committal because they did not know any more than the men did, but they could guess. So could the men.   They had all been through this sort of thing before, but this time it seemed different.

"I ain't never seen   this many Ts and LCIs together before."

"Me neither.   And all them ships!   What the hell's goin' on?"

"You know as well as me what's goin' on. Only I don't like the looks of it."

"It looks like they cleaned out the whole coast. There's Ts here from Milne Bay, Buna, Lae, Finschaven, all over the goddam place."

"A lot of them LCIs come from the same places. I remember some of them from down there."

"There's even boats here back from Biak and Noemfoor."

"And Sansapor."

"Yeah, it looks like everythings bein' collected here."

"I ain't seen none from Moratai."

"No, we won't see any that went that far north 'cause that's where we're goin' -   north."

"But there's nothin' north of Moratai but the Philippines."

"Jesus, the Philippines!"

"Forget it, these buckets could never make it there."

"They made it to Biak from here, and that's 300 miles."

"Yeah, and Moratai's a lot farther than that."

"Ya know how far it is to the Philippines? Manila's about as far from here as Brisbane is."

"I wouldn't mind makin' a run like that."

"Like what?

"To Australia."

"What would you do in Australia?"

"Are you kiddin'? There's beer and broads in Australia!"

"The beer's warm and the broads are cold."

"What the hell would you do with a broad? You've been out here so long you've forgotten what it's for."

"Oh yeah!"

"There's beer and broads in the Philippines, too."

"Yeah, that's right!"

"And booze!"

"Yeah, and booze, too."

"Jesus!"

"Do you really think these buckets could make it to Manila?"

"Well I'm goin' with 'em or without 'em."

"It's a helluva swim."

"Well it sure beats rottin' to death in this goddam place!"

"I've been on this flat-bottomed bastard for damn near a year and-a-half. Ya think I won't risk a little boat ride to get me some Filipino ass?"

"Now you're talkin'."

"Liberty in a real liberty port!"

"Manila was called the 'Pearl of the Orient' before the war."

"How come you know so much about the Philippines?"

"I read a lot."

"Booze, beer, broads!"

"And Japs, don't forget the Japs."

"Oh shut the fuck up! Why do you always have to piss on the parade?"

"There ain't no more Japs. MacArthur and Halsey's killed 'em all."

"In a pig's ass."

"I heard they caught one the other day in the chowline on Pancake Hill."

"No shit?"

"I shit you not. I heard it last night when I was on the beach.   This Jap got so goddam hungry that he actually tried to get a meal in the messhall."

"How hungry can you get?"

"He should've gone to MacArthur's place up on the hill. Mac would've made a houseboy outta him."

"Well pretty soon the Japs can have this whole stinkin' place back again.   There won't be nobody here in a couplea weeks."

"Ya   really   think   we're   goin'   to   the Philippines?"

"Sure we're goin' There ain't no other place to go, is there?"

"It figures."

"Sure it figures. Mac promised he'd return, didn't he? Well he's gonna return, and we're goin' to be right behind him as usual.   He couldn't go nowheres without us, could he?"

"No, he couldn't go nowheres without us dumb bastards."

"And he couldn't go nowheres without the **Nashville,** neither."

"Yeah, and there she is, Mac's private cruiser."

"When <u>that</u> baby comes into port ya know that somethin's up."

"Yeah, somethin's up all right."

"God 'elp us."

Chapter 4

A Briefing

Bell's boatload of officers was the first group to get ashore. They made their way to the cavernous messhall which had just been "secured" after serving breakfast to several thousand soldiers and sailors. Bell selected a table, sat down, and awaited the arrival of the rest of his officers. He scrutinized them as they entered.

How young they are, he mused. Dressed in their khakis, tieless, with their single gold or silver bars affixed to their wrinkled collars. College grads who had joined the Navy, gone to OCS for three months, were commissioned, and were then sent to join the Seventh Amphibs. Cruel jest. They had dreamed of action with the Fleet, only to find themselves in the flat-bottomed navy. They had vaguely heard of LCTs and LCIs, never dreaming that <u>they</u> might be assigned to the same.

As soon as they all had assembled, Lt. Bell rose and addressed the group.

"Gentlemen, may I have your attention. I have called you together this morning to tell you of Admiral Barbey's plans for us. No doubt you've been wondering about what the hell is going on. I'm sure that most of you have figured it out already. Well

I'm here to confirm your suspicions and to answer as many of your questions as I'm allowed to answer. First of all, we are leaving for Biak on the morning of the 13th of this month."

("We've been to Biak," said a voice from the audience.)

"We will stay there just long enough to top-off our fuel and water tanks for the second leg of the journey." (moan)

("Where to?")

"I cannot tell you at this time.   You will be told that at Biak."

("If we get to Biak. ")

"We'll get to Biak, and we'll get to our ultimate destination, too!" exclaimed Bell.

("What's the alternative?")

"The alternative is to stay here, in the brig!"

("How are we supposed to get to wherever we're supposed to go?")

"The LCIs will act as escort for the Ts."

("What will escort the LCIs?")

"An LST has been assigned to help us with any mechanical breakdowns that may occur along the way."

("How many are we allowed?")

"If any T has a complete breakdown it will be towed by an LCI."

("If!")

"Yes, and we'll tow every goddam one of them if we have to.   Now, are there any <u>intelligent</u> questions?"

"What about rations?"

"You will be issued whatever you need at the supply depot."

("<u>Whatever</u> we need!")

"Within reason.   We will not be carrying any cargo or troops, so load up with all that you need. Uncle Dan has passed the word that we are not to be stinted in any thing reasonable. This base will soon be a rear area, so load up."

("The condemned men ate a heary meal.")

"Goddamit, knock off those remarks.   If you have anything positive to say, stand up and say it."

"Lieutenant Bell."

"Yes, Williams."

"In view of the fact that we have very limited communications and aids to navigation, well, how are we going to do it?"

"The way we have always done it, Williams. My LCI will have the point.   You will follow me. We only have to make four knots to stay on schedule, so we can all be very close together. We will keep a very tight formation.   Straggling will not be tolerated.   We will have to be in visual contact with each other at all times.   And I don't mean with binoculars either.   I mean eyeball to eyeball."

"Will any lights be allowed?"

"Yes, running lights and a small red one on the stern of each vessel. You will have to stick your nose right up the ass of the ship ahead of you to keep that light in sight. Post a bow-watch every night to make sure that you don't lose sight of it."

"What formation will we sail in?"

"The Ts will sail five abreast in ten columns for as long as we can hold it. The LCIs will be on the flanks. The LST will bring up the rear at night. I"ll send you more detailed plans in a day or two."

"What if we have a breakdown during the night?"

("Mechanical or mental?")

"Standard operating procedure will be the same as always. If you have a breakdown you will lash your T alongside the T nearest to you. You will not stop! You will keep going until your own motor mac has cleared up the problem or until the LST can get to you. Whatever happens, there will be no stopping for anything. Is that clear?"

("Sounds like a jolly voyage.")

"Are there any more questions? No ? All right then. I suggest that you get back to your vessels immediately. Check all equipment and engines. Make all necessary repairs. Draw full rations, fuel, water, and in general prepare for getting underway on the morning of the 13th. You know what to do.

I'll try to inspect each vessel before we leave. I'll answer any specific questions at that time. However, if anything extraordinary develops contact me on the '34' with the light.   Good day, gentlemen."

"Attention!"

The officers rose.   Lieutenant Bell passed through them and returned to his ship.   And so began one of the most unbelievable voyages of World War II.

Chapter 5

"All Work and No Play . . ."

Gone were the days of equatorial slumber so enjoyed by our friend the Kookaburra bird. His laughter could hardly be heard above the man-made cacophony that had suddenly enveloped his favorite LCT. Never had he seen such frenetic activity. It unsettled him. Away he flew, never to be heard from again. However, he was not really missed by the crew of the 166. They were far too busy with other matters to notice the absence of a demented bird. Never before had their ship been given such a going-over.

All topside gear was being repaired . The engines were being overhauled. Cases of food and beer were being brought aboard. Even the flag had been replaced with a new one-piece model.

The ten-man crew was crawling all over the ship. No one was in the sack! Everyone had turned to in an orgy of activity completely foreign to their customary lifestyle.

Bosun Jazinski was roaring at Seamen Frisch, Mack, and Dugan to clean out the bosun's lockers on either side of the ramp. The cook and Seaman Pacelli were busy unloading an LCVP which had come alongside with a load of cases for the galley. The cases were temporarily stacked outboard of the bulwark on the catwalk until room could be found for them under the tarpaulin that was stretched forward of the crews' compartment.   However, a case of chickens and a case of beer were hustled into the refrigerator for more immediate consumption.

Motor Machinist Berger was up to his ass in grease and oil.   He and his "striker", Fireman Temple, had removed the small hatches over the engine room and were happily doing whatever it is that makes mechanics happy. The engine room on an LCT was located below and forward of the compartment.   It was about half the size of the compartment above and only about five feet high.   In that space were located three Gray Marine diesel engines.   Many a motor mac almost went mad in that heat and noise.   When all three engines were working properly (one day in May) they were capable of propelling the craft at breath-taking speeds.

Gunner's Mate Zale was busy dis-assembling and lubricating the 20mm guns while Signalman Essex was over-hauling the ramp winch.   That was not a normal duty for a signalman, but no one on a T felt stifled by being limited to just one specialty. Every man was expected to do whatever had to be done. These jobs were done with varying degrees of success, but they were done without any jurisdictional disputes.

All work stopped at four in the afternoon. Showers were taken, and all hands changed into a variety of clean clothes.   Then they ate a hearty dinner of fried chicken, re-constituted potatoes, canned string beans, and canned peaches.

"Eat them spuds," suggested the cook. "They'll put iron in your blood. They put iron in <u>my</u> blood. I can feel it."

"What you feel is the lead in your ass," countered the bosun.

In spite of everything, the cook was a good natured soul.   He was usually happy, which is a rare thing in a cook.   Well you'd be happy too if you were half full of "jungle juice" most of the time. He had the best "still" in the group. He could make booze out of anything.   "Brandy" was his specialty.   He could make "peach brandy" and "apricot brandy" or just about any kind of brandy you'd want.   As a result, he was a happy cook. The only thing that he was not really happy about was his stove.

"How the hell am I supposed to cook on a cast-iron stove fired by diesel oil?   I think they gave me a boiler by mistake and put my stove in the engine room of a battleship."

"Yeah, they put it in the **Arizona.** That's what blew her bottom out," said Seaman Mack unwisely.

"Stand up when you mention the **Arizona**, boy," growled the bosun. "I had friends on that ship."

"I'm sorry, Boats," Mack sputtered. "I didn't mean no disrespect." The bosun just glared at him.

"Hey, since we're all cleaned up and everything, why don't we go ashore tonight?" volunteered Seaman Frisch in an effort to change the subject.

"Oh I thought you'd never ask," mocked Berger.

"Why do we have to go ashore?" asked Zale. "We got beer here."

"We can look at the nurses and the WACs," ventured Essex. "We ain't got none of them here."

"We can go see the movie, too," persisted Frisch who did not like to go ashore alone because there were still Japs in the bush.

"Maybe Bob Hope's ashore," said Berger. "He ain't come to entertain us yet."

"He ain't comin'. He's in San Diego with Alexis Smith."

"I'd rather look at the broads, anyway."

"Come on, let's go," prompted Berger. "God knows when we'll get another chance to see a movie."

"What do you mean by that?" demanded the bosun. "Don't they have movies in Manila?"

"Yeah, sure, but we might not be goin' to Manila right away when we get up there."

"I thought we was goin' to Manila!"

"I don't know where the hell we're goin'. It might <u>not</u> be Manila for all I know. MacArthur don't let me in on his secrets."

"The fuckin' Japs'll prob'ly blow up the fuckin' movie house anyway," commented Fireman Temple. "They're always committin' outrages."

"Yeah, Temple's right," agreed the bosun. "That's just what them sonsabitches would do. God how I hate them bastards! All right, let's take the beer and go look at the broads and the movies."

A passing LCVP gave them a ride to the pier. Traversing the pier was difficult because of the bodies that had been placed athwart it to facilitate their identification and transport back to their respective ships. They were not dead; they were just dead-drunk. Many of them had come from off an Australian cruiser (HMAS Reprehensible) that was anchored in the bay. The custom aboard such royal ships is for the men to save their daily ration of the King's grog and then consume it all at once when they got ashore. They didn't go ashore to look at the ladies or to see the movie with a decorous beer or two, no, they went ashore to drink their rum. They sat on the beach in the sun wearing their proper uniforms and drank their rum, quickly. The combination of His Majesty's rum and the equatorial sun has a dramatic effect on anyone foolish enough to try it. However, the bodies observed on the pier that day did not appear to be especially foolish. In fact, they looked rather happy in their groggy state.

The walk up the hill from the pier to the outdoor movie area was tiring and thirst-provoking. Our merry band had to stop several times to refresh themselves from their dwindling store of lager beer which was rapidly turning tepid. They were also able to refresh themselves with a few glimpses of **real** women. They were wearing uniforms, but no matter, they were still the genuine article.

The movie facilities consisted of a projector, lights, seats made from the trunks of palm trees (a soft wood), and a canvas screen painted white and laced into a pipe frame. The featured film that evening was a June Haver special about a group of high school kids putting on a show to raise money for their local dog-pound. They still don't know how it ended, for right in the middle of this epic a large bush-rat attempted to scamper along the top of the frame holding the screen. Suddenly every GI in the audience who was armed stood up and opened fire on the rat. They shot the rat and the screen all to hell. That was the end of the movie for that evening.

"So what do we do now?" asked the cook when the lights came on.

"Ya goddam dumb sonsabitches!" yelled the bosun at the soldiers in the audience.

"Why'd ya do that for?"

"Take it easy, Boats," cautioned Essex, "they shoot Polocks, too."

"Oh yeah! Well if they'd shoot more Japs we wouldn't be sittin' in this goddam dump!"

A soldier staggered over to the bosun and asked, "You a Polock?"

"Yeah, what of it?" answered the bosun as he curled his right hand into a huge fist.

"Me too, I'm a Polock," smiled the soldier.

"No shit? Where ya from?" the bosun relaxed.

"Detroit," burped the soldier.

"No shit? I'm from Hamtramck, too."

"No shit? Well come along and have a drink with me and my buddies. Bring ya friends with ya."

And so off they went in the spirit of inter-service comaraderie that made America great and brought us victory in the late war in the Greater East Asia Co-Prosperity Sphere.

The next morning Gunner Zale was awakened by someone who was poking him with a stick. The sun in his eyes made it difficult for him to determine who his tormentor was, but he gradually ascertained that it was Ensign Smyth.

Looking about him, Zale espyed his shipmates laid out like ties on a railroad bed along the right-of-way of the pier. It was a memorable scene. Perhaps as many as a hundred bodies were spread the length of the pier.   Rank had no privilege there. Officers and men, soldiers, sailors, merchant seamen, but no women, were democratically intertwined in one long Grecian fresco.

Several officers and EMs were trying to unravel this Laocoon by poking and shaking familiar figures, turning them over, pulling at them, yelling at them. Their lack of consideration was not soon forgotten by the miserable miscreants moaning on the pier that morning.   However, those tactics did prove effective enough for Ensign Smyth to identify and rouse his ten charges, dump them into a boat, and get them back to the 166.   Once there, however, they were unable and/or unwilling to climb over the bulwarks of their nautical home.   So the ensign had to lower the ramp, thus making it possible for our gallant servicemen to crawl aboard.   After they were all aboard he raised the ramp again and left them to lie wherever they had fallen.

Later that day Lieutenant Bell came aboard to inspect the 166.   He took one look around and reminded Ensign Smyth that the convoy was leaving in three days, and if his T was not ready to go at that time he would have him courtmartialed!   At that moment the ensign suddenly realized why the Navy assigns officers to almost everything it has that floats.

"But for the young men who had never travelled far from home and had close family ties, the strain was terrific. There was no one to lean on. Assigned to a ship in the combat zone with limited water supply, stifling heat, lack of recreational facilities, crowded living space, little privacy, and intermittent bombings, the period of adjustment was a bit too much for some of them to bear. Terror, apprehension, home-sickness, all rode individually with these boys."

- Admiral Barbey

Chapter 6

Underway

13 October 1944

"Jesus!" exclaimed Seaman Pacelli. "Look at all them ships!" Every man on every craft in Lt. Bell's group was up at the crack of dawn that morning to watch Admiral Barbey's ships pass in review as they stood out of the bay bound for Leyte Gulf. Cruisers, destroyers, LSTs, minesweepers, tugs, patrol craft, oilers, and transports carrying the 42,000 men of the 24th Infantry and First Cavalry Divisions passed by. Similar scenes were being repeated at that moment all over the Pacific until the number of vessels bound for Leyte Gulf would swell to 738 ships of every type. That number included famed Task Force 38 which included 17 aircraft carriers, six new battleships, 17 cruisers, and 64 destroyers under the command of Admiral Halsey as part of the Third Fleet. This task force would fight the battles of the Sibuyan Sea and Cape Engano.

Admiral Olendorf's six old battleships, eight cruisers, and 20 destroyers under the command of Admiral Kinkaid as part of MacArthur's Seventh Fleet. This group would fight the Battle of Surigao Strait.

Also included was Admiral Thomas Sprague's 16 escort-carriers, ten destroyers, and 12 destroyer-escorts under the command of Admiral Kinkaid as another part of the Seventh Fleet. This group would fight the Kamikazes and the Battle off Samar.

In addition, there were the hundreds of planes aboard all of those carriers. That was the most powerful aggregation of sea power that that part of the world had seen up to that time. Approximately 165,000 soldiers and 50,000 sailors were aboard all of those ships.

The passing of Admiral Barbey's stately convoy was in sharp contrast to what followed as Lt. Bell attempted to get his convoy underway. The officers in charge of each of his 75 landing craft had been given specific instructions regarding their location in the formation. The LCTs moved with elephantine grace in attempting to follow the instructions. Eventually they did achieve a rough facsimile of their leader's intention.

LCT 166 found itself in the midst of a group of Ts five abreast. Ten such groups lumbered along in a tight formation as though in fear of losing sight of one another. The LCIs were lined up on each flank and ahead. The LST repair ship brought up the rear. So far so good, thought Ben Bell as his LCI neared Point Able.

Aboard the 166 Ensign Smyth had the wheel. Gunner Zale was in the house with him as was Motor Mac Berger. The crew had been divided into three "watch" groups. Thus the day was divided in sections of "four-on" and "eight-off", 24 hours a day in the ancient tradition of the sea. The cook and Berger did not stand regular watches because cooks don't, and the motor-mac would be on call 24 hours a day anyway. Ordinarily the captain of a ship does not include himself in a watch-section, but the 166 did not have enough "hands" to afford Ensign Smyth the luxury of playing the traditional role of ship's captain.

And so the shipboard routine fell into the hoary pattern of all ships underway - eat, sleep, and stand watch. However, aboard a vessel as irregular as an LCT it was a rare day when some tradition was not violated. The first day was typical because everyone was too interested in what was going on to spend any time in the sack.

"God but it feels good to be underway again!", exclaimed the bosun. "I don't care where I'm goin', just so long as I'm goin'." This feeling was shared by every member of the crew, and probably by every man in the group (except for those with a penchant for sea-sickness). Swinging on the hook was all right for a while, but being underway is what it's all about.

Always the quest, the yearning to be going to some new place. The horizon always beckoning with a tantalyzing promise of something new, something exciting. Something, anything, to break the boredom. And a sure cure for anyone's boredom is to sail through hostile waters. No, that's not the right word because the sea is always hostile wherever and whenever one ventures upon it. Or, as Victor Hugo said, "To be at sea is to be in front of the enemy. A ship making a voyage is an army waging war. The tempest is concealed, but it is at hand. The whole sea is an ambuscade."

If one can add to this the possibility of an encounter with a unit of the Emperor's Imperial Forces, then one comes up with a sure-fire cure for boredom. Anxiety and tension can also cause excitement of another variety. These last two elements were still dormant that first day of steaming northwest and away from Hollandia and its beautiful bay.

The weather that day was pleasant. The wind from the southeast gave the Ts a welcome tailwind, and such a wind against the large rectangular stern of an LCT was a force to be reckoned with.

"She handles well in a following sea," opined the ensign to his watch-mate Zale during the 0400-0800 watch.

"How can you tell at this speed?"

"Because the tank deck isn't bucking up and down like a whore in a Terre Haute cat house. That's how I can tell."

"You been to Terre Haute?" asked the suddenly interested Zale.

"I went to college in Indiana. We used to drive over there whenever we felt the urge."

"Yeah, I've heard about that place."

"They've got the biggest red-light district in the whole MidWest."

"No shit?   I'm from the East End of Long Island. We don't have nothin' like that."

"How old are you, Zale?"

"Nineteen.   I joined-up right out of high school.   I never got much chance to go cat-housin'. I never had much chance to do anything. My folks are very religious."

"I'm twenty-four," said Smyth. "I must really be the 'old man' on this bucket."

"No, I don't think so. Berger, and the bosun, and the cook are older than you.   The cook is definitely older than you. Cooks always look older. It's from all that jungle juice they drink. I never knew a cook or a painter that wasn't a rummy."

"Painters?"

"Yeah, house painters. Did you know that Hitler was a house-painter before he became a big

deal? Yeah, all those fumes from the paint, plus
the schnapps he was drinkin', messed up his head.
That's why this whole fuckin' war started, 'cause
Hitler painted houses. Ain't <u>that</u> a kick in the head?"

"Yes," laughed Smyth. "<u>That</u> is the most
original theory that I have ever heard, and it
certainly is a kick in the head."

At 0800 the four-to-eight watch was relieved
by the bosun, Seaman Dugan, and Fireman Temple.
Smyth and Zale went below to join Seaman Mack for
a breakfast of canned bacon, scrambled "eggs", toast
and coffee. The mess table was secured to the
forward bulkhead of the crews' compartment. The
men sat facing the bulkhead. The seats were app.
the size and shape of a tennis racket. They could be
swung out from under the table. The table itself
was about ten feet long and 18 inches wide.

Cooking is always difficult when a ship is
underway. A special grid is secured to the top of
the galley stove in order to keep the various pots in
their assigned stations. Even so, there is much
slopping about.

Eating is also difficult when a ship is underway.
Keeping a tray in front of you, and keeping a cup of
coffee from spilling while a ship is rocking and
rolling requires the skill of a prestidigitator.
Under such conditions speed is essential to the
successful completion of a meal.

An angry and a vengeful gut results from such eating habits and such a diet.

A popular mis-conception of sailormen is that the first place that they head for when ashore is a saloon. Not so. More than likely it's a restaurant. Saloons and women come later, in that order.

That first breakfast on their first day underway would have been a mercifully forgettable affair except for the presence of Seaman Mack at the table. Just by coincidence, the third member of the four-to-eight watch also hailed from the MidWest. Mack had been born and raised in Sidney, Nebraska. So naturally he was nicknamed "Sidney."

Sidney did not like to take showers, or to wash his clothes, or to eat with a knife and fork, or to discuss anything other than a woman's sex organs. His mattress and pillow were greasy-gray because he could not be bothered with a mattress cover or a pillow case. And he was always checking his crotch for "crabs" or any other exotic growth that might flourish in his curly-black mantle. It was not easy to offend the sensibilities of an LCTman, but Sidney managed to do it.

Sidney usually ate in isolation because nobody wanted to sit next to him, but at times it was impossible to avoid him and still get fed. That first morning was one of those unfortunate times. He usually ate at the end of the table near the hatch. That should have been Smyth's seat, but Sidney was allowed to sit there so that he could have the benefit of the extra ventilation. When Sidney prepared to sit down that particular morning he found that the ensign was occupying his accustomed place.   There was only one other space left at the table, and that was between Zale and Essex.   As Sidney motioned to sit between them Essex said, "Don't you sit next to me, you stinkin' sonofabitch!" This unequivocal statement put Sidney in a quandry. That was not the first time that Essex had called him that particular sobriquet.   The first time resulted in an altercation that left Sidney "nearer my God to thee."   He wisely decided that he had no other alternative but to take his tray outside and set it atop the gasoline-generator.   There his fumes mingled with those of the generator to produce an effluvium reminiscent of the stockyards of his youth. From then on Sidney ate most of his meals in the company of the insensate generator.   Sidney was happy, the rest of the crew was happy, but nothing was ever heard on the subject from the generator.

There was one exception to the above. Motor Machinist Berger was not at all happy about the new arrangement.   He kept a wary eye on his beloved generator and Sidney.   He was convinced that their source of electricity was in jeopardy.   If his suspicions had been confirmed then Sidney would have had to eat his meals in the "head."

After breakfast the Officer-in-Charge went topside to the bridge.   From that vantage point he could see the familiar curve of Humboldt Bay fading into the greater bulk of the island of New Guinea. Looking about him he could see that their armada was still holding a semblance of their planned formation.   None of the Ts had broken down as yet. Looking ahead he could see Lt. Bell's LCI in the lead. All's well at two bells, he thought.

However, the thought that was really uppermost in his mind at that moment was whether or not the plumbing in his private "head" would work, for he would soon have to put it to the ultimate test.   But the time for conjecture had passed!   A few minutes later a smiling ensign emerged from his private water-closet.   Multiple relief is a wonderful thing.

In the meantime, the bosun was giving Seamen Dugan and Fireman Temple a lesson in ship-handing in the wheel house.

"Now you gotta remember that this barge has three engines, three screws, and three rudders. It's like a Chinese battleship.   And them engines ain't turnin' that many revolutions, so ya really gotta lean on the wheel to get this bucket to go where ya want it to go. But all ya gotta worry about now is keepin' this bucket right behind that bucket ahead of us. Got that?"

"Okay, but what about tonight?"

"At night I'll have the wheel most of the time. You two will stand topside and bow watch. You'll relieve me every half-hour so's I can take a leak and get a cuppa coffee. It won't be no problem."

"What do we do on bow watch?"

"You keep your eye peeled on that red light ahead of us. If we start to drift off course you're to pound on the ramp with a hammer. The other guy on watch will go out to see what the problem is. Then he'll come back here to tell me."

"Hammer-navigation, that's a new one!"

"Not in this outfit, it ain't."

"But it's 300 miles to Biak!"

"Ah that ain't nothin'. A piecea cake. We went 400 miles from Milne Bay to Cape Gloucester durin' Christmas Week last year."

"What did you get for Christmas, Boats?"

"A new hammer."

"How long ya been over here?"

"I come over in 1942."

"Holy Jesus!"

"Yeah, I started in Australia - Brisbane. And it looks like I'm gonna ride this bucket all the way to Tokyo Bay."

"And you ain't been home in all this time?"

"No, I ain't been home, but I've been to

Australia."

"What's it like down there?"

"It's a fuckin' paradise, that's what it's like. When I was there those Aussie broads hadn't seen a man in so long it was murder."

"What do ya mean?"

"I mean that all of them broads hadn't seen a man in over a year because all the Aussies were over in North Africa fightin' the Krauts. Christ, it was heaven on earth.   All the pussy ya wanted, all the beer, you could drink , and then one night it all ended - sudden like."

"What happened?"

"One night the Aussies came back from North Africa without a word of warnin' to us. Late one night a couplea troop ships slipped into the harbor. The guys went home to surprise their families, and what do you think they found?"

"Oh no!"

"Yeah, they found Yanks in the sack with their women. The next mornin' there was dead Yanks all over the place. That was the end of the real good times Down Under."

"I never heard about that."

"Ya never heard of it because it was all hushed-up. How would that have looked in the papers? But it happened."

"Are they still pissed-off at us?"

"They was until we saved their ass at the Battle of the Coral Sea when we stopped the Japs from landin' on their north coast. After that we was all buddies again, but things was never really as good as they had been before."

"I hear they got great beer. That didn't change, did it?"

"No, that didn't change. It's still warm and strong. Three of their beers will knock you on your ass. They use <u>our</u> beer for chasers."

"I wonder if they make beer in the Philippines?" asked Temple who always had a great thirst.

"Sure they do, they must," answered the bosun with conviction. "It's a civilized country, ain't it?"

"But what if the Japs blow up the brewery?"

"Yeah, that's just what them sonsabitches would do," growled the bosun. "Oh well, even if they do, we've always got our own beer. This man's Navy floats on beer."

"Did you ever taste any Jap beer?" asked Dugan.

"Yeah, once in Finschaven."

"What's it like?"

"Tastes like warm piss."

"Well ain't that what Aussie beer tastes like, too?"

"Yeah, but <u>that's</u> Aussie-piss. Jap-piss is different. It melts ya teeth. That's why them Japs is so fanatical. They ain't got no teeth. They have to gum it to death," laughed the bosun.

The eight-to-twelve watch drifted on in the continuum of life aboard ship. Meals suddenly took on a more than normal importance. The men off-duty slept or lay in their racks watching the cook do his act. Actually his job was relatively simple due to the limited variety of food that was available for him to prepare. Chicken was the big item at that moment because it all had to be cooked before it spoiled. Clay was from the South, so he enjoyed frying the chicken. He was very good at it, too. The men were looking forward to lunch.

"Hey, Cookie," yelled Zale from his rack, "don't fry it in so goddam much grease this time, will ya!"

"Don't tell me how to fry chicken, ya goddam Yankee shit-kicker. I've been cookin' chicken all my life."

"Yeah, the same chicken."

"Why don't you show Pacelli how to do it?" asked Frisch. "He's supposed to be your helper."

"Gee, thanks Frisch," said Pacelli.

"He can help me by washin' the trays. I do the cookin'."

"But what if you get sick or somethin' and there ain't no one to cook?" asked Berger. "What'll we do then, starve? We got a long trip ahead of us."

"I remember once you were sick for three days," countered Zale.

"I wasn't sick, I was drunk. That's different. But I don't drink when we're underway. You know that."

"Yeah, but it's gonna be a long trip, and you might get tempted," said Berger.

"No, I ain't gonna get sick, and I ain't gonna get drunk neither unless you fuckers drive me to it."

"Hey Cookie," yelled Frisch, "next month's Thanksgiving. You gonna cook us a turkey?"

"Turkey! Where the hell am I gonna get a turkey? You must be outta your head."

"The last cook we had didn't cook us one neither,"said Zale, "so we chased his ass off the ship. I had to cook for two weeks while waitin' for you to show up. I've loved ya ever since, but you better cook us a turkey or there's gonna be trouble."

"Trouble?" yelled the cook. "You threatenin' me with trouble? Here we are in the middle of nowhere, surrounded by Japs, and you're threatenin' me with trouble! Man, you must be crazy!"

"Zale ain't crazy," said Berger. "He's just a little 'asiatic'."

"I'm no more 'asiatic' than you are, you crazy fuck! "

"Oh yeah? Then why do you spend all ya time readin' the same goddam magazine night after night?

The damn thing's fallin' apart. What are you gonna do when ya can't look at it any more?"

"I don't have to look at it; I've got it all in my head."

"What's so fascinatin' about that magazine?"

"There's a story in it all about college life," said Zale in a soft voice. "It tells how we can all go to college after the war on something called the G.I. Bill of Rights. The government will pay for it and everything. The article has pictures of girls on some campus wearin' skirts and sweaters and saddle-shoes and white socks. They're carryin' books and they stand around under the trees talkin' about things. And I imagine myself talkin' to them. I say, 'Hold on, Baby, I'm comin'. I'll be there one of these days. Don't go away. I'll be there under that tree someday with you'."

"In a pig's ass," replied Berger.

"Well, that's my dream, what's yours?"

"I don't have no dreams. All I have is nightmares. I'm trapped down in the engine room and no one can hear me screamin' because of the noise. I pass out with the heat. I fall on top of one of the engines. I burn up. All they find of me's a pile of ashes. That's my dream."

"Would ya like some 'peach brandy' when ya can't sleep?" asked the cook. "I always have some for 'medicinal purposes'. It'll help ya sleep."

"No thanks, Cookie. Sleepin' ain't my problem, dreamin' is."

"So Zale's gonna go to college and play grab-ass with the co-eds is he?" sneered Sidney. "And I'm the Queen of Roumania!"

"You smell more like the queen of the shit-house," snarled Zale as he made a move toward his antagonist.

"Zale is right," said Ensign Smyth as he suddenly emerged from his cabin wherein he had overheard everything. "The G.I. Bill is going to make it possible for every veteran to go to college. We're not going to be forgotten like the veterans of the last war. Zale's dream is very commendable. He will be able to go to college if that's what he wants to do. Cookie," he said after a pause, "what's for lunch?"

"Fried chicken, sir."

"Good, and next month we'll have a turkey, too, by God."

"Is that in the G.I. Bill, too, sir?" asked Berger.

"Not that I know of," laughed Smyth. "But I'll write to my congressman about it."

"Yeah, do that," said Berger, "and ask him about my discharge, too."

"Yeah," said Zale, a 'section-eight'. It's long overdue."

"Oh no, I'm not goin' to no funny-farm. I'm goin' to college with Zale."

"In a pig's ass!"

"I don't care how I get there," retorted Berger, "but I'm gonna be right behind you."

"You won't like Iowa."

"Iowa? What's that, a disease?"

"It's a state in the MidWest."

"Ya mean west of Jersey?"

"Yeah."

"Forget it," said Berger. "I'm never goin' west of Jersey again. This place is west of Jersey!"

"Chow down," yelled the cook. "The twelve-to-four watch eats first."

That watch-section consisted of Essex, Frisch, and Pacelli. After Essex and Frisch had eaten they went topside to relieve the eight-to-twelve watch. Seaman Pacelli stayed below to help the cook clean up. He rejoined the others after his galley chores were through. Pacelli had that duty because he was the newest member of the crew.

"How'd we ever get this lousy watch?" bitched Frisch as he sat on the deck of the wheel house while Essex stood behind the wheel. "This is the worst watch there is."

"Knock it off. It could be worse. You could be in the same section as Sidney. How'd ya like that?"

"Jesus, that's right! I couldn't stand bein' in here with <u>him</u>. I have to sleep near him, <u>that's</u> bad enough!"

"Well from now on he's gonna be on duty from four-to-eight twice a day. You won't have to see him, or hear him, or smell him for sixteen whole hours every day."

"Yeah, that's right. I don't feel so bad now."

"Go topside and take a look around. Maybe somebody's tryin' to get our attention."

Signalman Essex was probably the most essential member of the crew. He was the one on whom they all depended for getting the word and for passing the word. Ensign Smyth had a superficial knowledge of blinker and flags, but Essex was the specialist. He was an artist with hand-flags. Signalmen take pride in their style, and Essex had style. To see him pass the word was to see an artist at work.

Seaman Frisch enjoyed being on the bridge. He was young enough to imagine himself as Nelson at Trafalgar. His imperious gaze swept over the motley armada with a coolness that would have put the immortal admiral to shame.   He was shaken from his reverie by a loud voice from the LCT on the port side.

"Hey, give us a hand! We're havin' engine trouble."

Frisch reported this development to Essex who told him to report it to the ensign and the bosun. Soon the ensign was on the bridge. The bosun could be heard rousting out the crew with the immortal command, "All hands on deck!"

The bosun organized the rescue party with the utmost efficiency and profanity. First he ordered Sidney and Temple to get fenders over the port side to prevent the two vessels from beating each other to death. Then he ordered Zale and Dugan to pass a three-inch hawser up forward to secure around the forward bitts. Then he ordered Pacelli and Berger to do the same thing around the after-bitts. After these stations were manned Essex maneuvered the 166 alongside the ailing vessel and the two craft were lashed together. The other vessel provided the "spring-lines" to complete the securing of the two craft. The same operation took place on the other side of the ailing vessel. Thus it was helped along by its sister ships until its problem could be solved. Berger leaped onto the deck of the mid-ship to see what he could do to help.

Ensign Smith smiled at the self-suffiency of his crew. He had the utmost confidence that his vessel and the entire convoy would make it through to their ultimate destination.

The inconvenience of being lashed together three-abreast was not really an incovenience, for it was impossible to inconvenience the crew of an LCT. In fact, being lashed together was a <u>convenience</u> for it made it possible for the crews of the three Ts to intermingle.   They suddenly had different people to talk to, to exchange 'trade goods' with, to play with a new deck, to break the monotony.   It was suspected that some of the so-called breakdowns were mis-leading.   It may have been so, for practically every vessel in the convoy had at least one such experience.   They couldn't <u>all</u> have been that bad.   Well anway,they didn't slow the convoy down, and they undoubtedly helped avoid the few mental breakdowns that could have been expected on such a voyage with such heterogeneous crews.

In fact, it can be categorically stated that not one LCTman was any crazier when he arrived in the Philippines than he was when he left New Guinea.

Strangers were crawling all over the ship. The only men on duty were Essex, Frisch, and Pacelli.   Everyone else was having a good time visiting. Berger had disappeared in the bowels of the mid-craft. Seaman Pacelli was very upset.   He was the youngest and smallest member of the crew. He looked like an un-driven nail. LCTs were new to him. <u>Everything</u> was new to him. He never did adjust too well to life in the amphibs.

"Look at them crazy bastards!" exclaimed Pacelli. What they hell do they think this is - a block party? Where the hell's the captain?"

"Who's the 'captain'?" asked Frisch.

"Ensign Smyth," answered Pacilli.

"He went next door to visit," said Essex.

"Oh that's great! Even the officers are nuts!"

"What's the matter, Pacelli?" inquired Frisch. "Everything's all right."

"All right, is it?   What if a Jap submarine popped-up right now? What the hell would we do?"

"What could one Jap submarine do against all of us? He's only got a few torpedoes."

"They ain't gonna waste no torpedoes on us," added Essex.   "Do ya know how much them things cost? Anyway, we're unsinkable, so forget it."

"What about planes?" continued Pacelli.
"They could bomb the shit out of us."

"There's 200 20mm guns in the convoy," said Essex.   "No plane could fly through that amount of lead. Even so, the smoke from all them guns would hide us. You've nothin' to worry about."

"Oh yeah, well what about Jap ships? Destroyers, maybe," persisted Pacelli.

"There ain't no Jap ships down here. Have you seen any Jap destroyers, Frisch?"

"No, I ain't seen no Jap destroyers."

"There, ya see? There ain't no Jap destroyers around here or Frisch would've seen 'em. Right?"

"Right," laughed Pacelli, "but I still think you'r all nuts."

"Nuts are we?" exclaimed an angry Essex. "You ain't been out here long enough to see any real 'nuts'. We used to have a guy aboard named 'Poncho'. We called him that because he always wore a poncho, you know, foul-weather gear with a hole in the middle for your head. Well this guy always wore a poncho irregardless of what the weather was like."

"Why did he do that?"

"He was afraid of gettin' wet. When it rained he stayed in the bosun's locker. One day down in Saidor he run off into the jungle. We never seen him again. His folks was notified that he was 'missing in the line of duty'. He's prob'ly a chief in one of them tribes down there."

"Or maybe the Japs got him?" added Pacelli.

"You're really hung up on the Japs, ain'tcha?"

"You guys sound like ya never heard of Pearl Harbor!"

"Yeah, we hearda Pearl Harbor," said Essex, "and we've been to a lot of other places that you never heard of!"

"Well ain't you afraid of the Japs?"

"I don't worry about the Japs. I worry about the boredom, the heat, the rot, the engines, the food,and what's goin' on at home. I've got enough to worry about without the Japs. If I worried about them, too, I'd be with Poncho."

"Maybe they'll be some mail for us at Biak," said Frisch to change the subject.

"I don't want any fuckin' mail either!" said Essex. "The damn fools write all the wrong things. Their goddam letters tear me up more than anything else. Letters, for Chris' sake! Send <u>them</u> to the Japs, then the war would be over in a week!"

At 1600 hours they were relieved by Smyth, Zale, and Sidney. Smyth took the wheel. Zale went topside to stand look-out. Sidney stood relief until it was dark enough to go forward to stand bow-watch. Zale and the ensign swapped posts at half-hour intervals. Once it got dark Sidney would alternate as bow-watch and relief.

Everyone else, except Berger, had returned to the 166 to eat. The evening menu would feature fried chicken.

The sun set at 1830. Darkness enveloped them immediately. The inside of the wheel house went black except for the red compass light. Small running-lights were permitted on either side of the wheel house because of the proximity of no many vessels. Such lights could not be seen at any great distance. The bosun rigged the red stern-light.

Sidney went forward to sit on the port bitts. He had a hammer with him.

Tom Zale entered the wheel house. "Tell me your plans for college, Tom," said a voice from the dark.

"Oh, I don't have any real plans, sir. I just like to think about it."

"Yeah, I like to think about it, too."

"Well I don't know much about it. None of my people ever went to college. I was the first one in my family to graduate from high school. My folks don't have much money. I'm glad the war came along; it gave me the chance to get away from there. And now I guess it's going to give me the chance to go to college. It's funny how things work out."

"Yeah. I planned to get a teaching job in a small college in Indiana. I was going to settle down, get married, and teach English literature for the rest of my life. I'm not at all glad that the war came along."

"Well it can't last forever. One day you'll be able to go home and get that job. Maybe I'll be in one of your classes. Wouldn't that be a kick in the head?"

"I guarantee you an 'A' in the course."

"It will probably be the only one that I will ever get. Well, I'd better get topside for a look around. It's been nice talking to you like this, sir."

"The pleasure's been mine, Tom. Hold on to that dream."

"Yes, sir. A man's got to have a dream, especially out here."

"That's for sure; that's for damn sure."

At that moment Sidney burst into the wheel house yelling, "I'm gettin' all wet up there. I'm gonna get pneumonia."

"Fuck you," said Zale. "That's the first shower you've had in six months. It'll do ya good. It'll do us all good."

"Go get a poncho and put it on," said Smyth. "And then get back to your post."

"I ain't goin' back there to get pneumonia!"

"You've got a chance of getting pneumonia or a sure thing of getting a court martial," barked Smyth. "Which will it be?"

"Okay, I'm goin'. I was only kiddin'. You guys ain't got no senseayuma."

"We must have," said Zale, "to put up with the likes of you!"

"Well, ya won't have to put up with me much longer. I'm a goner."

"Then get gone and stop your bitchin'."

After Sidney had left, the ensign asked, "I wonder what his dream is?"

"Ask him the next time you see him. It'll make your hair curl. But don't worry, he won't ever show up in one of your classes. He's got a shovel waitin' for him when he gets home."

"Yeah, I can see him now sitting in the American Legion Hall back home snowin' all the old-timers with his tales of the South Pacific while he drinks their beer."

"He may even become the mayor of Sidney, Nebraska," laughed Zale.

"He can use that shovel for ground-breaking ceremonies."

"Oh my God, he's got to catch pneumonia."

On that happy note Smyth turned the wheel over to Zale. The ensign went topside to stand look-out for a moment. As he looked up at the Southern Cross he thought to himself, in a couple of days we'll cross the Line and never see these skies again. I wonder what else we'll never see again?

Chapter 7

Biak

16-17 October 1944

The convoy showed signs of a difficult passage as it entered the harbor at Biak. Several Ts were being towed by LCIs, and many others were lashed together. The brief lay-over there would give them time to make some repairs while their supplies of fuel and water were being replenished. Small yard-oilers and water tenders came alongside as soon as the Ts had dropped anchor.

"Where you guys been?" asked the man who was topping-off the fuel tanks on the 166.

"Oh some of us went to Noemfoor, some went to Sansapor, some went to Moratai, and some went to Australia for leave," lied Temple. But only the last part was a lie.

"Australia! No shit?

"I shit you not. Dugan here got a dose of clap to prove it. Don'tcha Dugan." Seaman Dugan was non-committal.

"No shit?"

"Show the man, Dugan. Don't be modest."

"Fuck you," he said as he walked away.

"A real dose of clap! Jeez, I ain't heard of anything like that in a long time."

"Be patient. We'll all get it when we get to the Philippines," predicted Temple.

"Ya really think so?" asked the oiler hopefully.

"Sure. The corpsmen are sharpening their needles right now."

"Jeez, I wish I was goin' with you guys."

"Do you know where we're going?"

"Don'tcha know? You guys are goin' to Leyte Gulf."

"Where's that, near Manila?"

"I don't know where the fuck it is! All I know is that we've gotta top-off every tank in this God-forsaken outfit in order to get you there."

"How far is it?"

"I hear it's about 900 miles."

"Nine-hundred miles! How the hell are we supposed to go 900 more miles?" Temple felt like crying.

"Beats the hell outta me, but that's what I heard."

A pall of gloom settled on Lt. Bell's group as the word spread among his small ships. Conversation ceased. Each man was alone unto himself with his heavy thoughts.

Ensign Smyth brooded on the bridge. When he finally raised his head he noticed a ship far off to the eastward. He trained his binoculars on it. It was an American warship which he could not identify at that distance.

"Hey, Boats," he yelled to the bosun down below,"come up here for a minute."

"What do you make of that?" he asked when the bosun had climbed to his level.   He took the glasses offered him and looked in the direction in which he pointed. "It's a cruiser." He studied it for a moment longer and then he yelled loud enough for everyone on the bay to hear, "It's the **Nashville**! It's MacArthur! He's on his way to Leyte Gulf!"

Pandemonium!   Suddenly all hands were topside fighting for the binoculars that would reveal the **Nashville** to them.   Wild yelling and cheering broke out.   Gone was the gloom that had pervaded the bay but a moment before. MacArthur was passing by on his way to the Gulf!   Their old spirit returned. No, it was more than that.   It was a spirit created by the mere passing of their legendary leader.   It was a strange love-hate relationship that existed between MacArthur and his men.   But beneath it was a pride in that man that could not be denied.   It certainly was not denied at that glorious moment in Biak.   MacArthur was on his way to Leyte Gulf!

"Fuck the 900 miles!" yelled the bosun. "It's a piecea cake!"   The men cheered him to the skies.

Bosun Jazinski was a Boatswain's Mate First Class U.S.N.   He was the only Regular in the crew. He was the senior petty officer on board.   He was in fact, if not de jure, the captain of the 166. Everyone deferred to him because of his experience, his physique, and his temper.   Not that he was a tyrant, he simply ran out of patience now and then. When that happened everyone gave him plenty of lee-way.

Jazinski had joined the Navy in 1934 at the age of sixteen in order to escape from Depression-ridden Detroit.   He loved the Navy. That was apparent as he grew from a skinny youth to become a six-foot 200-pounder.   His strength and girth were testimonials to Navy beans and beer.   He was an excellent seaman and a good shipmate.   The men liked him even when he growled at them. Growling was to be expected.   After all, he was a boatswain's mate in the Regular Navy!

The next morning the convoy got underway again.   Their course would be northwest from lofty Soepioro Point.   That landmark rises 2,500 feet above the sea.   It was to be their last sight of land until they neared Leyte Gulf.

The group was in much better shape due to its lay-over.   Most of the Ts were under their own power again.   A few still had to be towed, and a few were still lashed together, but the 166 was free of its port-side burden.

The eight-to-twelve watch had the duty. The bosun was at the wheel. Temple was standing lookout on the bridge. Dugan was in the wheel house with the bosun.

Seaman Dugan looked like a Norman Rockwell creation - curly red hair, green eyes, and freckles. He was only seventeen and slight of build, but he was as"salty" as anyone in the crew.

"We'll be crossin' the Line again soon," said the bosun. "Only there won't be any ceremonies this time."

"Yeah, we're all 'shellbacks' now, thank God."

"What's the matter," asked the bosun jovially, "didn't you enjoy the initiation?"

"Are you kiddin"?   They damn near killed me! It took me a week to get all that grease and graphite off.   Then I saw the bruises! They really gave me a goin' over.   And my head! Jesus, I was bald as a cue ball. No, I didn't enjoy the initiation."

"Yeah, it can be rough," sympathized the bosun, "but if you ever go south again you won't be on the receiving end."

"Why would I ever go south again?"

"Who knows?   You might get lucky and pull 'survivor's leave' in Australia."

"Jesus, that's a happy thought."

"Well, it's a one-way ticket to Australia or the States."

"Is that the only way to get out of this outfit?"

"It's either that, or get sick, or get wounded, or go nuts," explained the bosun.

"Not much of a choice, is it?"

"No, 'specially if you're nuts to begin with."

"Well I'd rather go back to the States than to Australia."

"Not me," said the bosun. "I'm goin' back to Brisbane after the war. <u>That's</u> the place for <u>this</u> Polock."

"How ya gonna get there?   Steal one of these buckets and sail her there."

"Why not? That's where these buckets came from.   And I bet I could find plenty of guys to go with me."

"Sure. Sidney would like to go."

"That's why I'm goin' south," laughed the bosun.   "The States ain't big enough for the two of us."

"Maybe a bomb will fall on him, and then we'll <u>all</u> get survivor's leaves. Wouldn't that be great?"

"That's no way for one shipmate to talk about another shipmate. But see what you can do about it. Arrange it with the Japs somehow."

"I've got a brother in the Fifth Air Force," said Dugan. "Maybe he'd do it for us."

"Sidney might get suspicious if you asked him to stand in the middle of a big red bulleye in the middle of the tank deck."

"Hey, that's a great idea! We've got enough red-lead in the paint locker to do it. Why not? We never use the stuff anyway."

"Have you any idea what a big red bullseye would look like from the air?" asked the bosun. "It would look like a big Jap 'meatball', that's what it would look like. The Japs would leave us alone, but our own planes would bomb the shit out of us. And you don't get survivor's leave if you're sunk by your own planes."

"Then I'll have to think of some other way of getting rid of Sidney," concluded Dugan.

"Can he swim?"

"No, I don't think so. He don't like water. But even if he could swim, who'd pick him up?"

"And the sharks sure as hell won't bother him."

"So let's dump him over the side," smiled Dugan. "He can drift back to Biak and everybody will be happy except the natives."

"Maybe a Jap sub will pick him up. They could use him for a torpedo. Sidney - the new secret weapon."

"The Geneva Code prohibits using Sidney for a torpedo," laughed Dugan. "That would be a crime against humanity!"

"Oh sweet Jesus," laughed the bosun. "I'll never see Brisbane again if I don't get away from these nuts! Get outta here, Dugan. I'm driftin' off course."

Chapter 8

The Battle off Samar

At this point in the story we are going to leave the crew of the 166 for a while to go ahead of them to see what was happening in and around Leyte Gulf at that time.

17 October 1942 - Three minesweepers began sweeping the approaches to Leyte Gulf. Units of the 6th Raider Battalion were put ashore on three small islands at the mouth of the Gulf. No prisoners were taken.

18 October - APD **Humphreys** delivered Underwater Demolition Team Number Five to determine whether the enemy had erected under-water obstacles to impale the landing craft of MacArthur's navy.   No obstacles were found.

19 October - Into the Gulf steamed Admiral Olendorf's Fire Support Group South to soften up the Dulag invasion beach.   Twelve miles north a similar demonstration was given by Admiral Wyler's Fire Support Group North off Tacloban.

20 October - The invasion of Leyte. MacArthur returned.

21-22 October - The expansion of the beachhead on Leyte.

23 October - Submarines **Darter** and **Dace** attacked Admiral Kurita's fleet in the Palawan Passage. They sank two heavy cruisers and damaged a third so badly that it had to be escorted out by

two destroyers. Thus were five ships taken out of Kurita's force threatening Leyte Gulf.

24 October - Light carrier **Princeton** was bombed and sunk. This in turn caused heavy topside damage and casualties to cruiser **Birmingham.**

The Battle of the Sibuyan Sea resulted in the sinking of the super-battleship **Musashi** by Halsey's flyers. The heavy cruiser **Myoko** was hit by a torpedo and had to retire to Borneo.

Halsey's Third Fleet was lured away from San Bernadino Strait to pursue Ozawa's decoy force off Cape Engano.

25 October (night time) -The American Navy was victorious at the Battle of Surigao Strait.

The morning after - The Battle off Samar. A detailed account of this battle follows because several of Bell's small ships were directly involved in the aftermath of this battle.

Two and a half hours after the cease fire in Surigao Strait another battle was shaping up 120 miles to the north, off the coast of Samar. Whereas the first battle had been a textbook classic in tactics, the second one was to develop into a melee.

At 0645 Admiral Clifton Sprague's six escort carriers (CVEs), three destroyers (DDs), and four destroyer-escorts (DEs) were about forty miles off

They had just secured from General Quarters. Their weary crews were relaxing over breakfast when lookouts reported anti-aircraft fire to the northwestward. Were our own ships firing at our patrol planes? Radiomen reported Jap gobbledegook on the air. Then the patrol planes reported spotting four enemy battleships, six heavy cruisers, and a dozen destroyers.

Admiral Sprague could not believe it! No one could believe it. Sprague asked for confirmation from his pilots. He received it from them and from his lookouts who had spotted "pagoda" masts poking over the horizon twenty miles to the northwest. Further confirmation was provided by multi-colored salvo splashes around Sprague's ships. Admiral Kurita's battered but still dangerous force had travelled 150 miles in five hours - completely undetected.

Kurita was even more surprised than Sprague. He thought that he had encountered Halsey's Third Fleet. In reality he had only encountered a portion of Admiral Kinkaid's Seventh Fleet. That portion had the voice radio call signal "Taffy 3."

Admiral Clifton Sprague was aboard Taffy 3's flagship, CVE **Fanshaw Bay,** on that fateful morning. He promptly changed course from north to east, rang up full speed (18 knots), launched his few planes, and ordered all ships to make smoke. He also sent an urgent message to Admiral Kinkaid down in Leyte Gulf. Kinkaid received that message at 0704.

The second shoe dropped at 0705 when he received an answer from Halsey to a question that had been sent him at 0412. That question had been added to a message concerning the action in Surigao Strait -

. . . IS TASK FORCE 34 GUARDING SAN BERNADINO STRAIT?

Halsey had not received this query until 0648. His reply was -

NEGATIVE. IT IS WITH OUR CARRIERS NOW ENGAGING ENEMY CARRIERS.

This was the first intimation that Kinkaid had that his northern flank was completely exposed.

MacArthur, Nimitz, Kinkaid, Sprague and everyone else had assumed that Halsey had left Admiral Lee at the Strait with Task Force 34 which consisted of six new battleships and concomitant cruisers and destroyers. No one but Halsey and his commanders knew that they had sailed off with all of the Third Fleet's 65 ships to pursue Ozawa's eighteen decoys. The coming of the dawn found Third Fleet 450 miles north of the waters off Samar. Admiral Toyoda's sucker plan had worked beautifully.

In the northern thumb of Leyte Gulf (San Pedro Bay) at that moment were General MacArthur aboard the **Nashville**; Seventh Fleet Commander Admiral Kinkaid aboard his flagship **Wasatch**; Admiral Barbey aboard his flagship **Blue Ridge**; and Admiral Wilkinson aboard his flagship **Mount Olympus.**

In addition to that distinguished company were 23 LSTs, two LSMs, 28 Liberty ships, one navy transport, and a protective cordon of DEs and various patrol craft.

On the beach at that moment were 132,000 soldiers along with 200,000 tons of their supplies and equipment.

And at sea at that moment were 75 LCTs and LCIs blissfully nearing Leyte Gulf.

All of the fighting ships of the Seventh Fleet had left San Pedro Bay to take up stations 100 miles to the south in Surigao Strait to prepare a reception for the expected arrival of Admirals Nishimura and Shima.

Admiral Kurita was to arrive elsewhere a bit later - unexpectedly.

The only sources of aid that could have helped Taffy 3 were Taffy 2 which was located some 60 miles to the south, and Taffy 1 which was located another 70 miles below that. However, they couldn't do much more than send their few planes to aid Taffy 3. The ultimate source of help were the heavy ships of the Seventh Fleet which were more than four hours away. But they were low on fuel and ammunition after just having fought the Battle of Surigao Strait. Regardless, four hours away was just too far away. The main part of the looming battle would be all over before that span of time had passed. Thus Taffy 3 was destined to bear the brunt of the attack with assists from equally weak and equidistant Taffies 1 and 2.

At the core of each of these three groups were six escort carriers nicknamed, "baby flat tops" and "jeep carriers." Each one was simply a flight deck secured atop a freighter's hull. Each carried 28 planes and boasted one 5" gun located in the stern. They had been designed for convoy escort duty and anti-submarine patrols. Their pilots were not trained to tangle with warships. Neither were the four destroyer- escorts in their protective screen expected to mix-it-up with the big boys. Only their three destroyers had been trained to attack men-of-war. However, that morning was not given over to debating the responsibilities of various ships and planes. The all went bald- headed for the enemy.

Admiral Halsey's startling reply to Kinkaid's query sparked a near-panic in Leyte Gulf. Seventh Fleet began a frantic search for fuel and ammunition.

Admiral Barbey reacted in the following way: "Hoping to save some of my force, I arranged to concentrate all Seventh Amphibious Force ships in shallow, narrow San Juanico Strait, which separates Leyte from Samar, with the slight hope that they would be out of reach of a raiding force."

Panic may too strong a word to use to describe the reaction to Halsey's reply that morning, but panic would be understandable in view of the fact that all that stood between Kurita's force and our drained forces in Leyte Gulf at that moment were the three Taffies.

At 0658 enemy battleships began firing at Taffy 3 from a distance of 17 miles. That was seven miles beyond the maximum range of the American guns. Less than a minute later 14", 16", and 18" shells began to smash into the sea around Taffy 3. Each shell weighed from one to one-and-a-half tons.

Their multi-colored geysers rose to a height of over 200 feet. Admiral C. Sprague was to remark later, ". . . it did not appear that any of our ships could survive another five minutes of the heavy-caliber fire being received . . . the ultimate in desperate circumstances prevailed."

At 0707 Admiral Kinkaid shot off the following message to Admiral Halsey:

ENEMY BATTLESHIPS AND CRUISERS REPORTED FIRING ON CTU 77.4.3 (Taffy 3) FROM 15 MILES ASTERN.

This message was sent in plain language (uncoded) but it was not received by Halsey until 0822. The delay may have been caused by the fact that Halsey was being deluged by messages from his own ships and pilots that had begun their action against Ozawa at 0630. It was reported that Halsey was annoyed by Kinkaid's messages. After all, it was not Halsey's responsibility to protect the Seventh Fleet. The Third Fleet was an aggressor force. Its function was to sink enemy ships, and that's exactly what it was doing that morning.

At 0725 Kinkaid fired another message to Halsey: CTU 77.4.3 UNDER ATTACK BY CRUISERS AND BATTLESHIPS. REQUEST IMMEDIATE AIR STRIKE. ALSO REQUEST SUPPORT BY HEAVY SHIPS. MY BATTLESHIPS LOW IN AMMUNITION.

This message was received by Halsey at 0900. Note the use of the word "request." Halsey was not under Kinkaid's command. Admiral Nimitz, back in Pearl Harbor, was Halsey's boss.

At 0727 Kinkaid tried again in plain language:

OUR CVES BEING ATTACKED BY 4 BATTLE
SHIPS, 6 CRUISERS PLUS OTHERS. REQUEST LEE
COVER LEYTE AT TOP SPEED. REQUEST FAST
CARRIERS MAKE IMMEDIATE STRIKE.

Halsey received this plea at 0900. The enemy
at that moment was in a state of confusion if not
desperation.   Apparently Kurita's judgment was not
what it should have been as a result of his being
without sleep for 72 hours, for instead of forming his
ships into a battle formation he gave the order for a
general attack.   This had the effect of putting each
of his ships on its own. But in spite of that order
his ships managed to improvise a "box" formation
wherein his cruisers formed one side of the box, his
destroyers formed the other side, and his battleships
closed the rear.   Through the open forward end of
the box he hoped to scoop up Taffy 3.

Providence came to their aid at 0706 in the
form of a rain squall that hid them from the enemy
for nine minutes. During that time every ship made
smoke. This combined with the squall to give them
an additional six minutes of obscurity. Admiral
Sprague ordered a course change from east to
south-southwest to being them closer to the
hoped-for relief from Leyte Gulf.

At 0720 Sprague ordered his three destroyers to attack the   six cruisers that were closing in on the carriers.   The DDs so ordered were the **Hoel** (CMDR L.S. Kintberger),   the **Heerman** (CMDR A.T. Hathaway), and the   **Johnston** (CMDR E.E. Evans). Each of these ships was less than a year old. They were fast (35 knots) 2,100-tonners of the Fletcher class. Each ship was app. 380 feet in length and forty feet in the beam. They carried five 5" guns in five mounts - two forward and three aft of the bridge. Their armament also included ten torpedoes which were fired from tubes . located amidships. Each ship carried a complement of 300 American sailors. That was their greatest strength.

As noted previously, Admiral C. Sprague had issued a   desperate order at 0720 committing his three destroyers to attack the six enemy cruisers. However, CMDR Evans on the **Johnston** had jumped the gun at 0710 when he told his crew "to prepare to attack a major portion of the Japanese fleet." The impetuous commander concentrated on the leading cruiser in the column - the **Kumano**. **Johnston** fired more than 200 rounds of 5" shells while closing to fire her torpedoes at the cruiser. The **Kumano** was hit by all of it. She dropped out of the fight. Then came the **Johnston**'s turn. She was hit by three 14" shells which tore right through her without exploding. Those behemoths were followed by three 6" shells which did explode within her. Those six shells killed or wounded half of her crew. One engine was knocked out causing her speed to fall off to 17 knots. Her "mattress spring" radar was hanging alongside the bridge where it had fallen killing three officers. She could no longer be steered from the bridge, so she had to resort to "manual steering aft" where orders were yelled down a hatch to blackened, bloody men who turned the rudder by hand.

During all of this CMDR Evans remained on the bridge of the **Johnston.** His clothes had been blown off from the   waist up revealing the barrel chest of his Cherokee ancestors. Two fingers of his left hand had been cut off by shrapnel. Regardless, he gave the order to fall in behind **Hoel** and **Heerman** to make another pass at the cruisers.

Planes from the three "Taffies" and Tacloban attacked in un-coordinated fury. They hit the enemy with torpedoes until they ran out; with bombs of all sizes until they ran out; with machine gun bullets until they ran out; and then they made dry runs on the Japs until their gas almost ran out.

The ships of Taffy 3 were . frantically zig-zagging, plunging through rain and smoke and geysers, desperately backing to avoid   collisions with their own ships; firing, screaming, burning, fighting to save their little carriers.

CMDR Kintberger decided that **Hoel** would attack **Kongo.** That battleship had apparently grown impatient at the back of the pack. It had charged ahead at 30 knots outboard of the cruiser column. Both ships began firing at each other when the range had closed to 14,000 yards. **Hoel** received a hit on the bridge which severely injured CMDR Thomas, the screen commander. This hit also knocked out her steering control. Steering was shifted aft to manual control. When the range had closed to 9,000 yards **Hoel** launched five torpedoes. **Kongo** managed to avoid those missles. She then fired a salvo at **Hoel** which hit her in the after engine room, knocked .out three gun turrets, and jammed her rudder. This put **Hoel** temporarily out of action. When she returned to the fight she attempted to get her remaining torpedoes into the **Hagaru.** That cruiser happened to be leading the enemy column at that moment. **Hagaru** was hit, but **Hoel** found . herself trapped between **Kongo** and the cruisers. With cannon to the right of her, and cannon to the left of her, she valiantly tried to fight her way out with only her two forward guns still in action. She was pulverized in that gantlet by more than forty hits. She went down quickly taking 253 destroyermen with her.

At 0735 Admiral C. Sprague sent the following to Halsey: UNDER ATTACK BY   BATTLESHIPS AND HEAVY CRUISERS.

At 0739 Admiral Kinkaid sent the following to Halsey: HELP NEEDED FROM HEAVY SHIPS IMMEDIATELY.

True, but where were they supposed to come from in time to help Taffy 3? Halsey may not have answered all of the pleas sent to him that morning, but God answered all of the prayers sent to him. His answer was, "God helps those who help themselves."

Heerman got into the second torpedo attack at 0750. In her eagerness to get into the fight she had steamed right through the carrier formation and then she almost collided with **Hoel** and DE **Roberts.** **Heerman** fired seven torpedoes at the **Hagaru** without any positive result.   She answered **Heerman** with fifteen salvos. Lucky **Heerman** had a charmed life. The only thing to hit her was some shrapnel from near-misses.   **Heerman** then turned her attention to **Kongo.** As she neared that ship she noticed three more battleships behind the first one! CMDR Hathaway climbed to the fire-control platform for a better look. He fired his remaining torpedoes at **Kongo** and then started peppering her superstructure with 5" shells. Soon the shells from <u>four</u> battleships were reaching out for **Heerman.** She wisely hauled out of there to return to the carrier formation.

Destroyer-escort **Roberts** (LTCMDR R. W. Copeland) was not as lucky. As a matter of fact, the **Roberts** should not even have been in that attack. She didn't know how to form up for a torpedo attack. She only had three torpedoes anyway. Her only other armament consisted of two 5" guns.But what she lacked in power she made up for in heart. Somehow she managed to get herself astern of **Hoel** and **Heerman** and ahead of **Johnston**. The brutalized **Johnston** did not have any torpedoes left. She went along just to provide fire support with her remaining guns.

At 0800 **Roberts** dashed to within 4,000 yards of a heavy cruiser and fired her three torpedoes. She stayed in close to infuriate her steel-clad opponents with gunfire from her two guns. For fifty minutes she frantically dodged, zig-zagged, and "chased salvos" in the belief that shells would not land in the same place twice. She was too small and elusive to hit until 0851 when she received her first blow. After that she reeled through the water from hit after hit. At the end of her gallant sortie only her Number Two Gun was still firing. The man in charge of that was Gunner's Mate Third Class Paul Henry Carr. Gunner Carr and his mates fired more than 300 rounds before the **Roberts** was dis-emboweled by 20 heavy shells. When she went down she took ninety men with her including Paul Henry Carr.

The other DEs in the screen were the **Raymond,** the **Dennis,** and **Butler.** It was then their turn to attempt to slow down the **Hagaru** and the other three cruisers which were inexorably gaining on the carriers. DEs against heavy cruisers! Such was the desperation that reigned that morning.

At 0730 the **Raymond** began firing her two 5" guns at the **Hagaru.** At 0808 she fired her three torpedoes without success. For another hour she continued to harass the cruisers. Only when her ammunition was nearly expended did she break off from the action. Lucky **Raymond** emerged without a scratch after spending ninety minutes in that chaotic arena.

The **Dennis** began her attack at 0740. At 0800 she ended the introductory formalities   by firing her trio of torpedoes. No hits were registered on the cruisers, but several shells landed on the **Dennis.** She promptly retired   at 0920 behind a   smoke screen provided by **Butler.** She took six dead and 19 wounded with her.

By 0826 **Hoel, Heerman, Johnston, Dennis, Raymond,** and **Butler** had fired all of their torpedoes. Within ninety minutes only four of those valorous ships would still be afloat.

At 0829 Kinkaid sent the following message to Halsey: SITUATION CRITICAL. BATTLESHIP AND FAST CARRIER STRIKE WANTED TO PREVENT ENEMY PENETRATION OF LEYTE GULF.

At 0830 he sent another message to Halsey: URGENTLY NEED FAST BATTLESHIPS LEYTE GULF AT ONCE.

At 0848 Halsey finally responded by sending the following to Admiral McCain of the Third Fleet: ASSIST SEVENTH FLEET IMMEDIATELY.

According to S.E. Morison: "McCain, fueling when he got the word, turned up flank speed and commenced launching at 1030 when distant 335 miles from Kurita. This was one of the longest range carrier plane attacks of the war; too long, for Avengers could not carry heavy bombs or torpedoes that far, and they suffered considerable loss without inflicting additional damage."

At 0850 Kinkaid sent the following to Admiral Olendorf in Surigao Strait: PROCEED WITH SEVENTH FLEET TO POINT NORTH OF HIBUSON ISLAND AND STAND BY. (This island is located at the northern end of Surigao Strait.)

By 0830 the **Hagaru** was so badly damaged by bomb hits from above and shell hits from below that she was forced to relinquish the lead of the cruiser column. Her place was taken by **Chikuma** followed by **Tone** and **Chokai**.

    Chikuma was promptly challenged by **Heerman**. The former responded by putting a salvo of 8" shells into the **Heerman** between her bow and her Number One Turret. The effect of this was to flood the **Heerman**'s forward section thus forcing her head down until her anchors were dragging in her bow wave. In spite of this, CMDR Hathaway did not reduce speed even though his ship was in danger of being pulled under. If he had slowed down he would have been destroyed by the passing cruisers. He continued to fight with his four remaining guns.

    Chikuma came under heavy air attack and pulled away. Her place was taken by **Tone** who also came under heavy air attack and pulled away. The **Chokai** was hit from above and was forced to join her battered sisters. **Chikuma** and **Chokai** were later to sink. This put the **Hagaru** back in the lead again. The remaining cruisers finally caught up with the American carriers.

    Admiral Sprague's flagship, CVE **Fanshaw Bay**, was struck six times. CVE **Kalinin Bay** was hit sixteen times. Their wounds were not mortal. However, CVE **Gambier Bay** went down after being holed by twenty 8" shells. App. 100 men went down with their ship.

In the meantime, CMDR Evans on the battered **Johnston** noticed that the enemy DDs on the other side of the box were finally coming to life. Four of them, led by the light-cruiser **Yahagi**, were forming up to make a torpedo run on the carriers. The commander decided that his ship would take them all on by herself. The **Johnston** bored in on the **Yahagi** in such a wild Cherokee attack that the disconcerted cruiser turned away. The sight of their departing leader prompted the following destroyers to fire their torpedoes prematurely at the carriers. CMDR Evans was "so elated that he could hardly talk," recalled LT Hagen (senior surviving officer of the **Johnston**). "He strutted across the bridge and chortled, 'Now I've seen everything!' " Not quite, for as soon as the enemy had fired their torpedoes they turned their guns on the **Johnston**.

At 0940 the **Johnston** could not absorb any more punishment. She went "dead in the water." The gallant ship was immediately surrounded by the destroyers whose torpedo attack she had spoiled earlier. They circled around her using tactics similar to those used by the Commander's warrior ancestors. At 0945 he gave the order to Abandon Ship. At 1010 she capsized, her long glorious agony at an end. A Japanese destroyer approached the site. The captain on the bridge of that ship was seen to salute as the **Johnston** went down. Fifty destroyermen went down with her, including Commander Ernest E. Evans who was subsequently awarded a posthumous Medal of Honor.

From high in the pagoda mast of his flagship Admiral Kurita looked out over a chaotic seascape. His destroyers were way off to starboard being harassed by the **Johnston.** His cruisers were way off to port being blasted by small ships and planes that just would not give up. The carriers were far ahead in the smoke and rain squalls. The only ships of his that he could see clearly were three confused battleships, three desperately wounded cruisers, and a wounded destroyer. His own battleship was the most confused because for ten minutes six torpedoes had chased his **Yamoto** north and away from the action and thus out of the battle.

Kurita's fleet was scattered over an area 25 miles square. The super-aggressiveness of the Americans had forced his ships to take such violent evasive action that Kurita had lost tactical control of his force. At 0911 he sent the following message to all units of his fleet:

ALL SHIPS GRADUALLY RE-ASSEMBLE. MY COURSE NORTH. SPEED 20.

Admiral C. Sprague aboard the **Fanshaw Bay** could not believe it - "At 0925 my mind was occupied with dodging torpedoes when near the bridge I heard one of the signalmen yell, 'Goddamit, boys, they're getting away!' I could not believe my eyes, but it looked as if the whole Japanese fleet was indeed retiring."

It took an hour for all of Kurita's ships to break off, turn north, and re-assemble.

At 0927 Halsey sent the following to Kinkaid: I AM STILL ENGAGING ENEMY CARRIERS. McCAIN WITH 5 CARRIERS 4 HEAVY CRUISERS HAS BEEN ORDERED TO ASSIST YOU IMMEDIATELY.

At 0935 Kinkaid sent the following to Olendorf in Surigao Strait: PROCEED NORTH WITH HALF OF SEVENTH FLEET.

At 1000 Kinkaid sent the following to Halsey: WHERE IS LEE? (Admiral Lee of Task Force 34) SEND LEE. .

At 1005 Admiral Nimitz in Pearl Harbor sent the following to Halsey: THE WHOLE WORLD WANTS TO KNOW WHERE IS TASK FORCE 34?

At 1015 the CVEs **Kitkun Bay** and **Saint Lo** were hit by kamikazes. Apparently there was to be no quick end to Taffy 3's agony.

At 1055 Kurita changed course from north to west-southwest for Leyte Gulf.

At 1110 CVE **Kalinin Bay** was hit by two kamikazes.

At 1115 Halsey sent the following to Kinkaid: TASK FORCE 38.2 PLUS 6 FAST BATTLESHIPS

PROCEEDING LEYTE GULF BUT UNABLE TO ARRIVE BEFORE 0800 TOMORROW.

At 1125 CVE **Saint Lo** sank. Rescue efforts began immediately and continued until 1535 when the last of the survivors had been picked-up. The ships involved in the rescue operation were the **Heerman, Dennis, Raymond,** and **Butler.** They pulled 754 men and officers from out the hungry waters off Samar. The four rescue vessels then turned south with their load of survivors. They sailed away with heavy hearts knowing that they had to leave hundreds of shipmates behind. Their ordeal was not to end for another two days and two nights.

At 1147 Kurita turned westward. At 1215 he turned southwestward again. At 1236 he turned north for the last time. For more than three hours he had been scuttling an erratic course while trying to make up his mind. A message from one of the few survivors of the Battle of Surigao Strait convinced Kurita that it would be foolish for him to continue on to Leyte Gulf. What would have been gained by sacrificing the remainder of the Imperial Navy in a gallant but futile sortie into the Gulf? No, what was left of the navy would have to be saved for the defense of the home islands.

At 1310 Kurita was back at the position where it had all started.

At 1315 Kinkaid sent the following to

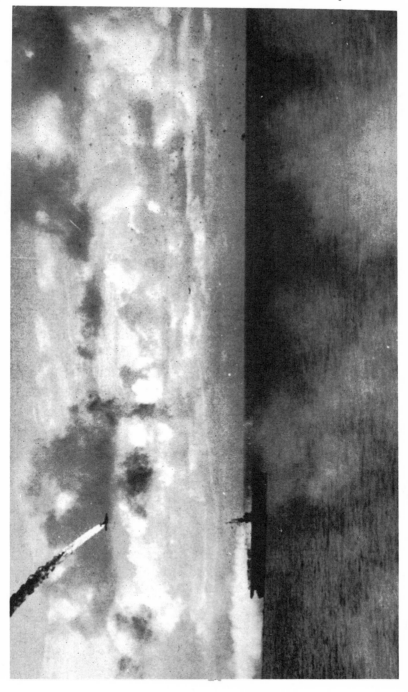

Olendorf: RETURN LEYTE GULF.

By 2130 Kurita was back in San Bernadino Strait with the remains of the most powerful gunfire force which Japan had sent to sea since the Battle of Midway. Their battle plan (Sho-1) had resulted in the loss of four of their carriers, three of their battleships, six of their heavy cruisers, three of their light cruisers, ten destroyers, and all of their planes and men. The once mighty Japanese Imperial Navy had been reduced to a third-rate status during three days and nights of fighting for control of Leyte Gulf.

Sho-1 had almost paid-off. It would have paid-off but for the courage and tenacity of the men of the U.S.Navy in general and Taffy 3 in particular.

For their tenacity and courage the officers and men of Taffy 3 were awarded the Presidential Unit Citation.

Taffy 3 lost five ships, 781 men killed, and 768 wounded.

Taffies 1 and 2 lost 283 men killed and 136 wounded.

In addition, 55 airmen were killed.   Nine of the wounded survived.

In all, 1,119 officers and men were killed and 963 were wounded.

Admiral Nimitz stated that "the history of the United States Navy records no more glorious two hours of resolution, sacrifice, and success."

The commanding officer of the **Hoel,** CMDR Kintberger, wrote the following tribute to his men: "Fully cognizant of the inevitable result of engaging such vastly superior forces, these men performed their assigned duties coolly and efficiently until their ship was shot from under them."

The commanding officer of the **Roberts,** LTCMDR Copeland, wrote the following tribute to his men: "To witness the conduct of the average enlisted man on board this vessel, newly inducted, married, unaccustomed to Navy ways and with the average of less than a years service, would make any man proud to be an average American. The crew were informed over the loud speaker at the beginning of the action of the Commanding Officer's estimate of the situation; that is, a fight against over-whelming odds from which survival could not be expected during which time we would do what damage we could.

"In the face of this knowledge the men zealously manned their stations wherever they might be, and fought and worked with such calmness, courage, and efficiency that no higher honor could be conceived than to command such a group of men."

Admiral Kinkaid stated, "That the **Johnston** should have been lost was among the calculated risks of such an undertaking. This ship did not go down in vain; largely through its efforts and those of the other ships the Japanese force was slowed down and turned back. What the Japanese had planned as an American naval disaster was turned into a Japanese rout. The part played by the **Johnston** in this cannot be over-estimated."

The following is from Commander Evans' Medal of Honor citation: "By his indominable courage and brilliant professional skill, aided materially in turning back the enemy during a critical phase of the action. His valiant fighting spirit throughout this historic battle will venture as an inspiration to all who served with him."

On the 25th of October in the year 1415 King Henry V of England faced an awesome French army on the field at Agincourt. This is what King Henry said to his men that day:

"This day is called the feast of Crispian:
He that outlives this day and comes safe home
Will stand a tip-toe when this day is named.
And rouse him at the name of Crispian.
He that shall live this day and see old age,
Will yearly on the vigil feast his neighbors,
And say, 'Tomorrow is Saint Crispian':

Then will he strip his sleeve and show his
scars,

And say, 'These wounds I had on Crispian's
day'.

Old men forget; yet all shall be forgot,

But he'll remember with advantages

What feats he did that day: then shall our
names . . .

Be in their flowing cups freshly remembered.

This story shall the good man teach his son:

And Crispin Crispian shall ne'er go by,

From this day to the ending of the world,

But we in it shall be remembered;

We few, we happy few, we band of brothers:

For he today that sheds his blood with me

Shall be my brother; be he ne'er so vile,

This day shall gentle his condition:

And gentlemen in England now abed

Shall think themselves accursed they were not
here,

And hold their manhoods cheap whiles any
speaks

That fought with us upon Saint Crispian's Day."

- Wm. Shakespeare

Chapter 9

Mid-Way

21-22 October

In the meantime, about 450 miles southeast of Leyte Gulf could be seen a sprawling, lumbering, gasping group of landing craft doggedly lunging ahead in a desperate attempt to stay on schedule. Their helpful tailwind had been chased away by a malevolent head-on northwesterly. The weather had turned grim and foul. One might even call it inclement. It was no time for a sailor to be at sea. But what could they do? They were at the point-of-no-return. The distance ahead was equal to the distance astern, so they might as well have kept on going.

"Why?" asked Seaman Pacelli in the wheel house of the 166. "If we turned around at least we'd have a tailwind."

"Turned around!" exclaimed Essex, " and how the hell do ya plan to turn this outfit around? It's hard enough just tryin' to alter course, without tryin' to turn around. No, this is a one-way outfit. There ain't enough water in this God-forsaken ocean to give us enough sea-room to turn around in."

"That's right," said Seaman Frisch from the close darkness of the wheel house. "We're always goin' in the same direction - northwest. We're prob'ly magnetized because we're always pointin' that way, like the compass. Northwest is the only way we can go!"

"Maybe the cook's right about us havin' iron in our blood. That's why we're magnetized!" said the impressionable Pacelli.

"How far can we go in this direction?" asked a worried Seaman Frisch.

"All the way to China," answered Essex as he stood at the wheel.

"I don't wanna go to China," said Pacelli. "I want to go to Japan and hump them Geisha girls."

"You gotta be kiddin'," said Essex. "Do you really think them Japs are gonna let the likes of you get at their women? More than likely they'll make chopped suey out of your ass and jam it down ya throat?"

"Chop Suey ain't Japanese, it's Chinese," cook's helper Pacelli informed them with a knowledgeable smirk.

"Oh yeah," laughed Essex, "well it's gonna be Itralian by the time they're through with you."

"Yeah, we better go to China," said Frisch very seriously. "I don't wanna mess with no more Japs. Ain't there no end to them bastards? Ain't there no end to this goddam ocean and these goddam islands? Seaman Frisch was starting "to crack." He was a 19 year old native of Minnesota whose people still spoke German at home. He was subject to the melancholy inherent in people of northern-European descent. In appearance he resembled a blond beer barrel. He would be a very dangerous person to be near if he got violent.

"No, this ain't never gonna end," said Essex, "but I've got an idea how to get out of it."

"How?"

"Did you guys ever hear of the Northwest Passage?"

"No."

"Well it's somethin' that explorers have been lookin' for for a long time. It's supposed to be a short-cut to the Orient."

"So?"

"So we're headin' for the Orient, ain 't we?"

"Yeah."

"And we're always goin' northwest, ain't we?"

"Yeah."

"Well then!" exclaimed Essex.

"Well what?"

"We've found it, ya dummies. We've found the Northwest Passage - the shortcut outta here. Whadda ya think?"

"I think you're nuts," answered Pacelli. "The only way outta here is . . .

"Yeah?"

"There ain't no way outta here," moaned Frisch. "We ain't never gonna get outta here. Us and the Flyin' Dutchman. We're gonna be here forever."

"Fuck the Flyin' Dutchman," said Essex. "We'll be in Leyte Gulf in four days. And if they hit the beach yesterday like they was supposed to then the area will be secured by the time we get there."

"Jesus, just think of it," enthused Pacelli, "liberty with real women!"

"Aint'cha gonna miss them black broads down in New Guinea?" joked Essex.

"I never had nothin' to do with them broads," exploded Pacelli, "and you know it!"

"They was gettin' whiter every month," said Frisch.

"We got you out of there just in time,kid,"said Essex. "Them broads would've murdered ya."

"I'm savin' it for my girl back home," volunteered Frisch.

"And who's she savin' it for?" asked Pacelli.

"I didn't know ya had women in Minnesota," said Essex. "I thought you only had Eskimos."

"Well I wouldn't mind havin' one of them Eskimos right now," sighed Frisch.

"You better stop sighin' and get your ass up forward," said Essex, "before the 'old man' finds out that nobody's watchin' his red light."

"I can see it from here," said Frisch. "Anyway, we've got a deal worked out."

"Who's got a deal?" asked Essex.

"Me and the guys on the other Ts. Since there's three of us lashed together again there's no sense havin' three guys on bow-watch at the same time, especially in this kind of weather. So we trade off every half-hour. It's my turn in about ten minutes."

"And what about you, Pacelli? Ain't you supposed to stand lookout or somethin'?"

"I was on lookout. I'll tell ya what I saw. I saw 24 LCIs towin' 24 LCTs. All the other Ts are lashed together. There ain't a single ship sailin' alone except for the '34' and the LST. It's a very depressin' sight. I don't wanna look no more."

"Well you gotta look!" yelled Essex. "Someone might be tryin' to get me on the light. Here, take the wheel, I'll go topside."

"Okay," said Pacelli, "but just take a quick look around."

"You'll never make third-class with that attitude," growled Essex. "Frisch, get up forward!"

"Yes, sir!" mocked Frisch. "And when I get my 'crow' can I yell at the seamen, too?"

"You're a third-class seaman now. What more do ya want?" replied Essex angrily.

"I wanna be a cox'un, then I can yell at you," responded the ingenuous Frisch.

"The last cox'un what yelled at me   was left with a mouth fulla loose teeth! So get your fat ass up forward before I kick it up there!"

Frisch departed.

On the morning of October 22 the word was flashed from the '34' that fuel from the totally incapacitated LCTs was to be pumped into adjoining Ts that still had one or more engines working.

Half of the LCTs were arranged in groups of three with the helpless Ts in the middle. The outboard vessels each had one or more engines working thus making it possible for them all to maintain the crucial four knots. And making it all possible was the repair ship making its endless rounds.   If it hadn't been for that ship and its tireless crew the pathetic convoy would never have made it to Leyte Gulf on time, if at all.

LCT 166 still had two of its engines functioning on the morning of the 22nd. She was located outboard of the helpless 181.   The 204 was outboard of the 181 on the other side. She also still had two engines still in operation. This threesome was barely able to maintain the required speed thanks to the heroic ministrations of their motor macs and their helpers.

Berger and Temple were constantly nursing their mechanical charges. Temple was relieved of watch-standing so that he, along with Berger, could give his full time and attention to the engines. Never were Gray Marine diesels more carefully tended.   Never were motor macs more highly regarded.   Everyone suddenly became very solicitous of Berger and Temple.   They enjoyed a status never to be achieved again after that particularly anxiety-ridden voyage.

"Three more days to go," yelled Berger as he leaned over a partially dis-membered Number Two in the engine room.

"Yeah, and don't forget the nights," yelled Temple in an unsuccessful attempt to be heard over the roar of the two remaining engines.

"What?" yelled Berger.

"Let's get outta here for a while," yelled Temple.

"Okay," yelled Berger.

When they got topside they sat down on the wet-cool tank deck with their backs against the steel bulwark.   They were silent for a moment before Berger yelled, "How's the fuel holdin' out?"

"Ya don't have to yell now, Dave.   We're topside."

"Oh.   Yeah.   That's right.   How's the fuel holdin' out?" he asked in a more moderate voice.

"Fine. The 181 has more than enough to get us there."

"Where?"

"Leyte Gulf. Don'tcha remember?"

"Oh yeah, Leyte Gulf," Berger mumbled. "That's somewheres up north, ain't it?"

"Yeah, Dave. It's in the Philippines. Just three more days, like ya said, and we'll be there."

"What're we supposed to do when we get there?"

"I don't know ," replied Temple. "Finish repairin' Number Two, I guess."

"Yeah, that's right. Finish repairin' Number Two."

"And don't forget, Dave, there's women and booze in Leyte. We're gonna have us a good time up there."

"Yeah, we're gonna have us a good time up there," repeated the exhausted Berger.

"Ship me somewheres north of Biak, where the best is like the worst; where there ain't no Doug MacArthur, and a man can drown his thirst."

"Hey, that's good; I like that," said Berger. "Ship me somewheres north of Biak, ship me somewheres . . ."

Temple got the bosun to help him put Berger in his rack ·

Fireman Temple was a 21 year old from

Tampa, Florida. He was "striking" to achieve the rate of Motor Machinist's Mate Third Class. He was very close to achieving his goal. If he and Berger could keep their engines running for another three days and nights they would both receive a jump in rate.

Frank Temple had spent a great deal of his young life fighting people who wanted to nickname him "Shirley." As a result of this experience he was very good at street fighting. The only one on the 166 who tried to nickname him was Sidney. No one tried it again after the failure of that initial effort.

Frank was six-feet tall , weighed 180 pounds, and wasn't about to let anyone call him Shirley.

After he and the bosun had put Berger in his rack, Temple said, "The poor sonofabitch ain't had much in the way of sleep since we left Hollandia."

"Well, let'm sleep the clock 'round if he wants," said the bosun. "If anything serious goes wrong we can hail the repair ship."

"He won't like that," said Temple. "He said he don't want no deck apes messin' with his engines!"

"They ain't deck apes," yelled the bosun. "They're all motor macs and 'lectricians, like him."

"I tell ya he don't want them fuckin' with his engines. He's gonna be real pissed-off if that happens."

"Well that's too fuckin' bad, ain't it! What are we 'sposed to do, fall out because he don't want no strangers messin' with his engines? Fuck him!"

"What's the racket all about?" moaned the cook from his rack. "How's a guy 'sposed to get any sleep with you garillas makin' all that noise?"

"Fuck you, too," soothed the bosun. "Get your ass out of that sack! We're gettin' hungry."

"I don't feel good."

"He's been at the brandy," said Dugan.

"Oh he has, has he? And what the hell are we 'sposed to do for chow? Where's Pacelli?"

"He just got off watch."

"Well that's too fuckin' bad, ain't it? Wake him up!"

"You wake him up," answered the fearless Dugan.

"I'm up," yelled Pacelli from his rack. "Who could sleep in this riot?"

"Get breakfast ready," ordered the bosun. "Evers is drunk."

"Fuck him, that's his job," replied Pacelli.

"When Evers gets drunk he stays drunk for three days," explained the bosun in a low voice. "He won't know the coffee from the ketchup until we get to the Gulf. So you're gonna do the cookin' till then. Understand?" he said as he curled his right hand into a fist.

"What about my watches?" asked a deflated Pacelli.

"Ain'tcha learned nothin' yet about this man's navy, ya dumb dago dope?   Cooks don't stand watches!"

"Oh, all right then," said the new cook as he climbed out of his rack.

"What's for breakfast?" asked an amused Dugan.

"How the hell do I know?" retorted Pacelli. "I don't even know how to light the goddam stove!"

The bosun pointed out the valve that controlled the flow of oil into the firebox. He inserted some paper, lit it, and closed the firebox lid.   "There, that's all there is to it."

"It's a marvel of efficiency," mumbled the cook from his observation post.

"Oh shut the hell up, ya goddam rummy," sympathized the bosun.

Evers went back to sleep. That put two members of the 166 on the inactive list.

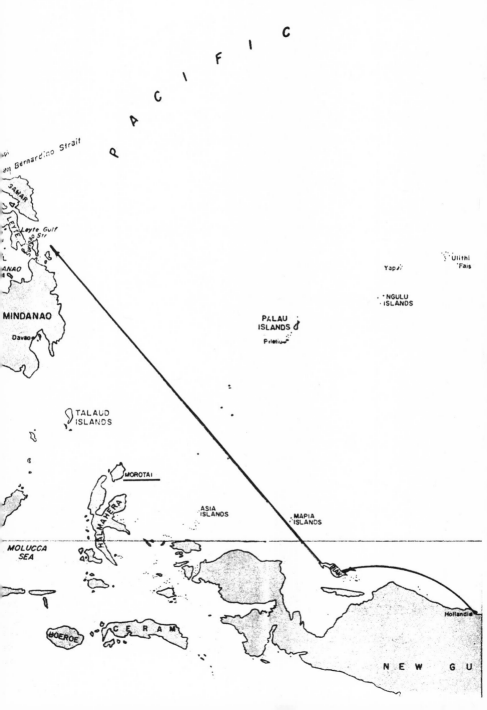

In the meantime, Lieutenant Bell was also having his problems on the leading ship (LCI 34). He and two other officers, Ensigns Willis and Anderson, had the full responsibility of navigating for the entire convoy. They led the way, but at that particular moment they were not too sure of the way. Overcast skies for two days had prevented them from taking a "shot at the sun" with their sextants. They had to rely solely on their one compass, their single chart, and their instincts.

"Well, if we keep on going northwest we're sure to hit land," said Willis.

"That's comforting," said Anderson.

"The Malays used to navigate these waters by the stars," said Bell.

"They obviously knew something that we don't," said Willis. "Celestial navigation is beyond me."

"We should have stopped off at Morotai to shanghai a Malay navigator," said Anderson.

"Yeah, that would have made more sense than this straight shot from Biak to Leyte," replied Willis.

"There wasn't any time for that," laughed Bell. "We're just going to make it as it is."

"So what's the rush?" asked Anderson. "The invasion took place two days ago."

"Uncle Dan told me to get there on the 25th," said Bell, "so we're going to get there on the 25th."

"Well, we might make it alone," said Willis, "but have you noticed what's following us?"

"Yeah, the sad sacks of the Seventh Amphibs," said Anderson.

"Every LCI but ours is dragging a T behind it. Do you really think that we're all going to make it to the Gulf?" asked Willis.

"Yes," answered Bell. "We're all going to make it to the Gulf, and to Manila, and to Tokyo itself if necessary. And I don't want to hear any more of this negative talk. We have a big enough burden to drag without that, too!"

"I wonder what it's like on one of those Ts after a few days underway?' mused Willis.

"It's goddam unpleasant, that's what it's like," answered Bell. "You two have been spoiled with this LCI duty. You should try the Ts for a while."

"No thank you," said Willis. "This is bad enough." There was a pause, and then he asked, "I wonder how they will act when they get to the islands?"

"What do you mean?" asked Bell.

"I mean when they get ashore."

"They'll go ape-shit. That's how they'll act. What do you expect?"

"As officers are we supposed to do anything about it?" asked Willis.

"No, there's nothing that we can do until they get it out of their systems," replied Bell. "Most of those men have been cooped up on those barges for damn near a year and a half. The only thing that's keeping them going is the thought of having a good time when they get to Leyte. If you try to deny them that then you're really going to have trouble on your hands."

"But we have to have some control over them, don't we?" asked Willis. "I mean that it's part of an officer's responsibility, isn't it?"

"Control them during the day when there's work to be done," said Uncle Ben, "but let them be at night.   It will be rough for a few days, but once they've gotten laid, and drunk out of their minds, they'll be all right again. There's going to be the goddamdest party that you've ever seen when those men get ashore.   It's too bad that we can't join them."

"But I thought that rank had its privileges," said Anderson.

"Perhaps, " said Bell, "but I'm afraid that we will have to wait for ours. An officer is supposed to be a gentleman, and a gentleman is supposed to be discreet. So we will just have to wait until such an opportunity presents itself."

"I don't want anything to do with those native girls anyway," said young Willis. "I'm engaged."

"That's all right," said Anderson.   "Just remember what Kipling had to say on the subject - 'The things that you learn from   the yellow and brown will help you alot with the white'."

FIDELITY

E.A. Wilson

The following originally appeared in **Men, Ships, and the Sea** by Captain Alan Villiers:

"I led my odd ships (LCIs) down the channel at Bermuda, formed them up with difficulty and headed east . . .

"Most of the time I was glued to my bridge - three steps across and two back, with a compass and a couple of voice pipes. The steering was below in a protected wheel house. There was no other armor except gun shields.

"I kept the column wide and short so I could control them. In blacked-out nights I couldn't see them, and by morning some vessels would not be there. It is a scary thing for a young watchkeeper to keep station all night jammed in among 24 ships. The one ahead is too close; suddenly it looks frightening. Its wake is right in your bow wave! And the dark shapes on each side are veering off course, yawing to slice right into you!

"I had been briefed that a 40 percent loss was not only acceptable but almost expected."

Chapter 10

The Rescue

25-28 October 1944

Lieutenant Bell's group of landing craft approached Leyte Gulf at the time when the Battle off Samar was raging to the north of them.

Bell's group attracted a good deal of attention from Taffy 1's pilots. They could not believe what they saw below them in that early light. For there below, covering a square mile of the Philippine Sea, was the sorriest collection of ships that they had ever seen. But by God they were all there! Every one of them that had left Hollandia two weeks earlier was about to enter Leyte Gulf on schedule!

A signalman on a nearby escort carrier began to communicate with the signalman on LCI 34. Everyone in the group tried to follow their laconic conversation -

CVE to LCI: Identify yourself (pause) What is your destination? (pause) Hostile aircraft and ships in the area. Good luck.

Lieutenant Bell told his signalman to swing his blinker light from east to south. He had the following message sent to his group: Battle stations. Full speed. Follow me.

The early morning light also illuminated the disconcerting sight of a score of Liberty ships fleeing southeastward and away from Leyte Gulf.

Bell's group witnessed the first organized Kamikaze attack of the war. They were about ten miles north of Taffy 1 when they saw it get jumped by six planes whose pilots had one-way tickets. The CVEs **Santee** and **Suwanee** were hit, they did not sink; however, they did leave a lot of smoke on the horizon in addition to 283 dead and 136 wounded. Thus was the Navy introduced to what was to become the scourge of the Pacific Fleet - the planned Kamikaze attack.

Our landing craft were inside the Gulf when Admiral Olendorf received the order to assemble the Seventh Fleet north of Hibuson Island. A destroyer in the vanguard of the fleet challenged our intrepid group as it attempted to pass north of the same island. An angry blinker-light demanded the identity and destination of the group. It did not end its interrogation with a friendly admonition. Instead, it told them to get the hell out of the way.

"Whadda they think we're tryin' to do?" yelled the bosun as he stood behind the wheel of the 166. "We ain't no 30-knot destroyer squadron for Chris' sake!"

The crew of the 166 was at battle stations. Temple was strapped into the 20mm gun on the starboard side of the wheel house. Sidney was his loader. Frisch was strapped into the other gun.

Dugan was his loader. Gun Captain Zale was sitting on a "ready box" smoking a cigar. The recovered cook was standing by the fire hoses. The recovered Berger was listening very carefully to his choleric engines. The remainder of the crew was in the wheel house. No one was smiling. The conversation went like this:

"I thought this place was supposed to be secured by the time we got here?"

"That's what I was told," replied Ensign Smyth.

"Some security! The Japs are hittin' the carriers; the freighter's are haulin" ass like there's no tomorrow, and the whole fuckin' navy's off our port side lookin' real mean and nervous! What the hell's goin' on ?"

"The Japs must've pulled a fast one."

"When? Now. Jesus. Where we headed? San Pedro Bay. Where's that? Up ahead. How much longer? Who knows. Holy shit! "

At 0953 Admiral Olendorf was ordered to steam north with half of the Seventh Fleet.

The conversation among the gunners went like this:

"Don't look now, but the whole fuckin' navy's sailin' across our wake!"

"What the hell's goin' on?"

"Who knows?"

"They had a whole goddam week to secure this goddam place!"

"Yeah, and now here <u>we</u> are in the middle of Shitsville!"

"Maybe we should've got here sooner to take care of things."

"Yeah, one look at us and the Japs would've hauled ass."

"I wish to hell <u>we</u> could haul ass."

"Well we can't, Sonny. We're stuck but good in this goddam mess."

"We should've hailed one of them freighters."

"One of them was the **Alex Smithers.**"

"I've got a big picture of it stoppin' for <u>us</u>."

"She's half-way to Australia by now."

"And <u>we're</u> half-way to San Pedro Bay, wherever <u>that</u> is."

"That's the end of the line, Sonny."

"Stop callin' me Sonny!"

"Rest and recreation in a Jap prison camp."

"Oh shut the fuck up and keep your eyes peeled for Jap planes!"

"How we 'sposed to know if they're Japs or not?"

"If they shoot at ya, shoot back."

"They won't shoot at us. We look too much like the Jap navy."

"We look more like the Hungarian navy."

"Yeah, and they'll make goulash out of us if they get the chance."

"You're a cheerful sonofabitch, ain'tcha?"

"So what's to be cheerful about, you dumb bastard?   We're sailin' right through the middle of no-man's-land and he wants me to be cheerful!"

"I come up here for beer and broads, not to get my ass shot off!"

"I promised ya beer and broads, and that's what you'll get."

"More likely it'll be sake and geishas."

"I'll settle for that."

"More likely it'll be queers and cokes."

"I'd settle for anything to get out of this place. Oh why did I ever leave home?"

"To see the world."

"Pretty soon we oughtta be seein' the old **Blue Ridge** again.   Then everything'll be all right."

"Yeah, Uncle Ben won't let us down. Everything'll soon be all right."

"Yeah, everything'll be all right," they said as they scanned the skies.

At 1315 Admiral Olendorf received the word that the Battle off Samar was over.   The survivors of the **Saint Lo** were being rescued at that moment. But the survivors of the **Hoel, Johnston, Roberts,** and **Gambier Bay** were still in the water.

By 1700 Bell's group finally arrived in San Pedro Bay. LCI 34 was promptly met by a Patrol Craft. Bell was taken to the **Blue Ridge** to report to Admiral Barbey. The weary group of landing craft dropped their anchors in the shallow waters of the bay. Half of the men remained at Gereral Quarters. Enemy aircraft were still making things hot in the area.

While Admiral Barbey was congratulating Bell upon his singular achievement he was handed a message from a pilot who reported that he had seen hundreds of men in the water off Samar. The message contained their position. The pilot noted that there were no ships in the area.

Admiral Kinkaid had received the same message. He ordered Admiral T. Sprague to release some of his escort vessels to search for survivors. DEs **Eversole** and **Bull** were sent on that search, but they did not find any survivors because the position reported by the pilot was incorrect. Their true position was from 20 to 40 miles northwest of the reported position.

"No ships in the area of survivors!" exclaimed Admiral Barbey. "Well we've got plenty of ships <u>now</u> for such work thanks to Lieutenant Commander Bell here. How many of them are fit to go out again, Ben?"

"You mean <u>now</u>, sir?"

"Yes, now."

"Well, I'm not sure, sir."

"We'll only need about half a dozen LCIs. That should be enough. Shouldn't it, Jim? (The admiral here addressed LTCMDR James A. Baxter who was to lead the rescue flotilla.)

"Yes, that should be enough. But we don't know for sure how many men are out there."

"The dispatch said 'hundreds'."

"Each LCI can carry about 200 men," said Baxter, "so six should be enough."

"Even five would be enough," said the admiral.

"Yes, sir."

"Five LCIs plus two Patrol Craft should be able to do the job, right?"

"Yes, sir."

"Okay. Ben, get back to your group and pick out five LCIs for this detail."

"What about LCTs, sir?"

"No, they're too slow."

"We're short of fuel, sir."

"I'll have the yard oiler come alongside. You can go back to your group aboard her. In the meantime I'll get Kinkaid's OK on this."

"And what about provisions, sir."

"You'll only be gone for a day or two. You'll have to get along on what you've got. If we wait to get you completely outfitted there won't be any reason left for your going out there. Do you get my meaning?"

"Yes, sir.   And what about doctors or corpsmen?"

"You can have Doctor Lucas and a few corpsmen from this ship."

"Thank you, sir."

"Okay.   You've got an hour to select your LCIs, get them re-fueled, and get them back here. Any more questions?"

"No, sir."

"Good.   I'll have the oiler hailed for you immediately."

"Thank you, sir."

"Get those men, Ben.   If you and Jim don't get them, nobody will."

"We'll get them, sir."

"Good. Get cracking!"

With that ringing in his ears, Ben Bell went to the gangway to await the arrival of the oiler. Before long it arrived flying its tattered red flag. Bell was soon making the rounds of his LCIs looking for five that still had some life in them. He selected his own 34, the 71, the 337, the 340, and the 341. They were promptly fueled and sent alongside the **Blue Ridge**.   They were joined by two Patrol Craft - Baxter's 623 and the 1119.

By 1830 the new group had Kinkaid's blessing and an official designation - Task Force 78.12.   It also had its own flagship - PC 623. And it had its own Task Force Commander - LTCMDR Baxter. Our new LTCMDR Bell felt a little uncomfortable in the real navy.

Doctor D.B. Lucas went aboard the "flagship" accompanied by three Pharmacist's Mates - William Wattengell, James Cupero, and Otis Miller. Those four men were to perform medical miracles before that voyage was over. Miracles were sorely needed to supplement the lack of medical supplies and facilities ordinarily needed to care for hundreds of stricken men.

Shortages of all kinds existed in that improvised mission of mercy. There were not any extra blankets, or clothing, or provisions. But whatever they had would be given to the survivors off Samar.

At 1900 the seven small ships departed San Pedro Bay at a speed of nine knots. They were bound for an erroneous position 125 miles away. It would take them 14 hours to get there.

By 1900 the remaining survivors had been in the water from eight to ten hours. Most of the seriously wounded were dead by then. But there were still hundreds of them trying to stay alive in the waters off Samar.

LCIs to the Rescue

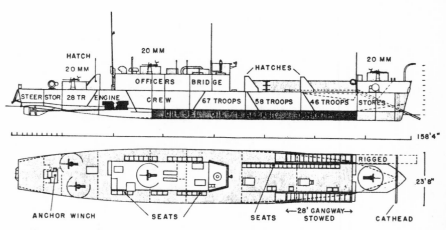

An oceangoing infantry carrier designed for direct unloading onto the beach, with a capacity for six officers and 182 enlisted men. It carries four 20-mm. guns. Dimensions: length, 158'5½" o.a.; beam, 23'3". Speed: 14 knots maximum.

How can one describe the agony endured by those men? Almost all of them were either wounded, burned, shell-shocked, or any combination of the three. How can one describe the agony of a gaping wound or a third-degree burn exposed to oil-covered sea water?

Some of those men had to wait for 50 hours before relief finally arrived. Most of them had to wait at least 40 hours. Relief came sooner for many of them.

How can one describe the hours between sunset on the 25th and sunrise on the 26th? Hundreds of men abandoned in the darkness and silence of the shark-infested Philippine Sea, each one of whom deserved a Navy Cross, left to drift for themselves on that now forgotten battlefield. Below them rested the hulks of their five brave ships containing the remains of their shipmates. They were to be joined by others who slowly spiraled downward through the black water off Samar.

How can one describe what that long night must have been like for the seriously wounded men, aboard the rafts? Those with just "ordinary" wounds and burns depended on their life-jackets to support them. Those that had passed beyond the pale of human endurance took off their jackets and attempted "to swim home." Others tried to beat their brains out on floating debris. Some succeeded.

Some were taken by sharks.

How can one describe the sounds that must have passed over the water that night - the screams and moans, the prayers and hymns, the babbling and the insane laughter?

How can describe the hunger and the thirst? How can one describe the effect of ingesting a gut-full of salt water and fuel oil?

How can one describe the effect of helplessly watching one's friends die and slip away beneath the surface of the indifferent sea?

How can one describe the hope and frustration of seeing planes and ships without being seen in return?

And then the coming of daylight and the roll-taking. The living replacing the dead aboard the rafts. The blinding sun in the east. The broiling sun overhead. The mocking beauty of the sunset. And then <u>another</u> interminable night in the cold water off Samar.

October 26

Task Force 78.12 reached its pre-determined position at 0830. All engines stopped. Every man became a lookout. They drifted upon the spot indicated on their charts. They silently gazed over miles of empty ocean. In reality, they were 25 miles southeast of where the **Gambier Bay** had gone down.

LTCMDR Baxter figured correctly that wind and current must have carried the survivors westward. He had his ships fan out in line abreast with one-thousand yard intervals between ships. They began making north-south sweeps on 25-mile legs working westerly toward the coast of Samar. No aircraft were sent out to help them.

The following is a summary of some of the log entries made aboard Baxter's ships:

0910 Sighted several planes and ships. Unable to contact due to sun and distance. Have received no information relating to survivors.

1049 Passed through oil slick. (The dead ships were still bleeding down below.)

1400 Three seaplanes passed abeam two miles.

1440 Sighted airplane belly tank off port bow.

1445 Sighted three unidentified aircraft dead ahead.

1500 Passed through heavy oil slick.

1645 Sighted object in water. It appears to be a survivor.

1659 Sighted 50-cal. ammo box; also two belly tanks and numerous boxes.

1700 Picked up Japanese survivor. He was kept afloat by holding onto a wooden box.

1716 All ships coming about to search area again.

1812 General Quarters. Ack-ack off port bow.

1820 Sunset. Darkened ship.

1848 Secured from General Quarters.

2127 Sighted much debris and heavy oil slick. Completed investigation of objects in water. No sign of life.

2220 Sighted red, white, and green flares bearing 270 degrees. Investigating flares.

October 27

The flares were twenty miles to westward. By midnight the rescue ships were among the survivors of the **Gambier Bay.** They had drifted 30 miles. In another couple of hours they would have drifted onto the beach of enemy-held Samar.

AT 0348 Patrol Craft 1119 was detached to return to San Pedro Bay with some 200 of the most seriously injured men.

Between midnight and sunrise on the 27th the task force had rescued app. 700 men of the **Gambier Bay** including her captain.   Fifty men had died in the water.

At sunrise the six remaining ships   continued their north-south sweeps of the area. At 0745 they sighted the first survivors of the **Hoel.**   Their position was app. 12 miles northeast of the first group of survivors. At 0800 they sighted the first survivors of the **Roberts.** At 0900 they finally came upon the survivors of the **Johnston**

There were only 282 survivors of the **Hoel, Roberts,** and **Johnston.** There could have possibly been 160 more if the navy had made a concerted effort to rescue them. There would not have been any if they had remained in the water much longer.

By 0936 the search was over. Not another living soul could be seen. Approximately 980 officers and men had been rescued thanks to that diminutive task force.

The TF was back in San Pedro Bay by 0150 on the 28th. By 0230 the men were being transferred to the temporary hospital ships LST 226 and LST 464. The next day they began being transferred to regular hospital ships and to other medical facilities throughout the Pacific.

Upon being released from hospital the men were sent home of 30-day survivor's leaves. Most of them never again had to sail westward under the "bridge of sighs" that spans the entrance to San Francisco Bay. Never again were they called upon to play David to the Japanese Goliath. And forever after they would be marked by a certain detachment from other men who had not been with them on that Crispin's Day off Samar.

Chapter 11

"Victory, Joe"

The crew of the 166 had mixed emotions as they watched   the five LCIs sail away on their rescue mission.   They would have willingly followed Uncle Ben if they had been chosen to do so, but they were also glad to have finally dropped anchor in San Pedro Bay.

The morning light of the 26th of October revealed the following disposition of ships in the bay - 23 LSTs, two LSMs, one APA, several DEs, four PCs, 50 LCTs, 20 LCIs, the repair ship, and the **Blue Ridge.** So many ships presented a tempting target to land-based aircraft.   They were constantly buzzing the ships, Tacloban, and the surrounding countryside. Condition Two (half the crew at battle stations) was the order of the day.   The ships departed as soon as possible for other anchorages.   As their number declined so did the number of air attacks. Eventually the remaining ships could secure from Condition Two.

The enemy became discouraged with the slim pickin's and by the increasing number of defenders rising from Tacloban's soggy air strip. They went after bigger game elsewhere.   And so did the war, as elusive and unpredictable as a typhoon, moved off to other waters and other shores.   The most desperately fought- over prize of the Pacific war had had its week of agony and glory. Never again would Leyte achieve its pre-liberation lifestyle. Never again would it recapture the rapture of its former torpor. The Japs had been chased into the hills and off the seas. The Yanks had arrived!

Now let us return to the bridge of the 166. It is the morning of the 27th of October.

"That ain't Manila, is it?" asked the bosun as he surveyed the debris-strewn beach, the blasted palm trees, and the pall of smoke hanging over Tacloban.

"No," replied Berger, "that can't be Manila. It ain't big enough."

"Then where the hell are we?"

"We're in San Pedro Bay."

" I know we're in the goddam bay, but what's that town over there?"

"I don't know."

"Go wake up Smyth; he might know."

"No. Leave him alone," said Essex. "There's only one way to be sure and that's to go ashore."

"But we ain't got a boat!"

"What do ya call this?"

"We can't take this ashore without orders!"

"So who's to give orders?" asked Essex. "Smyth's unconscious, and Bell is long gone. Who knows when Smyth'll wake up or when Uncle Ben will return? In the meantime we need supplies, don't we? And the only place we can get them is where the army is, and that's on the beach!"

"What about that APA over there?" asked the ingenuous Frisch. "Maybe they'd give us some."

"That's the navy, ya dummy," said Zale. "All they'd give us is orders."

"Fuck that," explained the bosun. "Let's go ashore."

Even the sound of raising the anchor did not awaken the somnolent Ensign Smyth. Berger goosed the engines just enough to give them the power to put them on the beach. The ensign slept on. The landing was as soft as a baby's butt. The ramp was slowly lowered. They had returned!

Essex, Berger, Zale, Frisch, and the bosun were about to tip-toe ashore when Zale suddenly realized that they looked more like natives than sailors. The stealthily returned to the compartment to search for dungarees, denim shirts or T-shirts, white hats, and GI boots. The remainder of the crew slept on. The cook was snoring loudly.

"Should we take rifles?" asked Gunner's Mate Zale when they had re-assembled on the tank deck.

"Yeah, that's a good idea, helmets, too," concurred the normally reckless Essex. "There's still Japs out there."

"There is?" said Frisch.

"Yeah."

"Then count me out. I don't want to get my ass shot off."

"Okay," said Essex. "You explain everything to Smyth when he wakes up. Tell him that we went 'foraging' and that we'll be back soon."

"Okay," replied the relieved young seaman.

And so the four-man landing party went ashore to explore the enchanted island of Leyte. They had to walk a tortured mile to the Tacloban pier that had accommodated the General's PT-boat a few days earlier. They duplicated his triumphant tour by walking from the pier toward the Tacloban City Hall. The main street was mud churned by hundreds of military vehicles and thousands of soldiers. The buildings on both sides of the street were all without roofs or glass in the windows. But most of their blackened walls were still standing thanks to their solid brick construction.   New roofs were being built in the old style using bamboo beams and palm thatch.

The four sailors created a stir as they walked up the road.   Native children escorted them yelling, "Victory, Joe!   Two cigarettes." When the cigarettes were not forthcoming their dialogue changed to, "You no fucking good, Joe,"   and other prime examples of hastily   learned GI English.   However, our foursome had not gone ashore to study local dialects. Their interests lay elsewhere.   Elsewhere suddenly appeared in the form of a crudely lettered sign which proclaimed, "Ramon's Bar and Restaurant." And in smaller letters "Ramon Vargas, prop."

They promptly entered the establishment to be met by a radiant entrepreneur who spoke a unique brand of English.

"Welcome, my friends, welcome. I am Ramon Vargas. This is my bar and restaurant, but today is your bar and restaurant. Have whatever you want with no payment."

"Well that's very nice of you," replied the well-mannered Zale. "What do you have to drink?"

"Tuba," replied the publican.

"What's that?" they all replied.

"Fermented coconut juice."

"Is that all you've got," asked the disappointed bosun.

"Yes. I hope to get some whiskey and beer soon, but tuba is all for right now."

"Okay, we'll try some of that stuff."

Ramon went to the bar to find four mis-matched glasses into which he poured a clear liquid from a gallon jug. The men then sampled their first drink of "Tuba."

"Tastes like perfume," said Berger.

"Tastes like it'll take the top of your head off."

"Sip it, lads, sip it. We're in uncharted waters," cautioned the bosun.

The fearless four relaxed. They took off their helmets, placed their rifles against a wall, sat down at a table, leaned back and surveyed the area. Ramon's emporium was about as long and as wide as an LCT. It was also roughly divided into three sections as was a T. The first section was the bar area up forward. The restaurant area was located mid-ships. The cooking was done over an open fire in a pit located to one side of the eating area. Chickens had the run of the place thus announcing the specialty of the house.

Ramon invited the men to move to the rear of his establishment so as to get away from a crowd of curious Filipinos that was standing six-deep in front of the open window. The after-section to which they were led contained a room furnished with a sofa and two rattan chairs which were padded with cushions! There was also a rattan coffee table, a corner table, a lamp, and a radio. The rear wall was open to provide access to a small private yard.

"Hey, this is great!" exclaimed the impression-able signalman.

The others shared his enthusiasm. They hadn't seen such luxury since they had left the States. Berger turned the radio on. The sounds of a Glen Miller recording poured into the room. The men froze.

"Jesus," one of them said reverently.

Moonlight Serenade was followed by the voice of a Japanese announcer: "This is Radio Manila saying sayonara to the hundreds of American sailors who are drowning at this moment in the waters off Samar as a result of the historic victory of the Imperial Navy. To their memory I dedicate the following recording of **Bye, Bye Blues.**"

Berger turned the radio off.

"Here we sit laughin' and scratchin' while hundreds of our guys are dyin' out there," said Zale. "It kinda takes the fun right out of it, don't it? Come on, let's get outta here."

"Relax," said Berger. "That's just Jap propaganda No one's dyin' out there 'cause that's where Uncle Ben went with those LCIs. He's prob'ly got them all picked up already. Let's have another drink. There's nothin' we can do about it anyway."

"Yeah, what the hell. There's nothin" that we can do about it."

"Well I don't like it," continued Zale. "Sittin' 'round here doin' nothin' while everyone else is doin' somethin'."

"Like what?"

"I don't know, but they ain't sittin' here."

"All right, all right, we'll go," said the bosun. "But the next time that ya turn on the radio, Berger, will ya make sure we ain't tunin' in the Japs!"

Ramon was upset at their premature departure until Berger told him that they might return that evening.

"Why'd you tell him _that_ for?" asked Zale once they were out in the street.

"Why not? It's possible."

"Well if we do come back I'm bringin' my own beer," said the bosun. "I ain't drinkin" no more of that panther-piss."

"Yeah, maybe we can trade him some beer for some good stuff and for somethin' to eat."

"All he had was chickens. Ain't you had enougha _that_?"

"I wonder where they keep the girls?" mused Essex out loud. "That's what _I'd_ like to know. I ain't seen an signs of pussy, have you?"

"They ain't exactly tacklin' us in the street, are they?"

"Not exactly."

"Ya know," said Berger as they walked along the edge of the beach, "I wouldn't be surprised if we was gonna need some _money_ in this dump!"

"Maybe not," replied Zale. "Maybe we can get by with trade goods."

"These people don't need beer and cigarettes," said Essex. "What they need is food and clothing. And we don't have none of _that_ to give away."

"Yeah, we'll have to wait for a freighter," added the bosun.

"So what are we gonna do in the meantime?" asked Berger as he stooped to pick up a coconut.

"We'll just have to use what we've got," said Essex. "Whatever we have is a luxury to these poor bastards."

"Emilio didn't look so poor."

"No, he ain't, but the rest of them sure as hell are."

"How come he ain't poor, too?" asked Zale.

" 'cause the Japs like to eat and drink, too, dummy."

"Then fuck him," offered the bosun. "I ain't tradin' with no collaborator."

"Yeah, fuck him."

The walk back to the 166 was very wet and very hot. They began to feel the effects of the small quantity of tuba which they had drunk.

"Jesus," said Zale. "I'm sure glad that I didn't drink any more of that stuff. I'm beginnin' to feel it already."

"It's the heat."

"I've been hot before, but I never felt like this before."

"Maybe that collaboratin' bastard poisoned us!"

"Yeah, let's go back and take the place apart," suggested the bosun.

"Later," said Essex. "We're almost home now."

The 166 was still on the beach. It had attracted a crowd of Filipinos. They were all over the ship. The delinquent quartet had difficulty getting through them.

"Where the hell you been?" screamed Ensign Smyth when he espyed his missing crew members. "I ought to have you guys court-martialed! Get these people off the ship, then I'll court-martial you. Let's get off this beach!"

It took about 15 minutes to clear the deck, raise the ramp, and back-off the beach. Then Smyth read the Riot Act to the un-authorized liberty party.

"The next time you guys pull a dumb stunt like that I'm gonna have you thrown in the brig so long your teeth will fall out! You're goddam lucky that Commander Bell isn't here or your ass would be mud!"

"Commander Bell?" asked the bosun.

"Yes, Uncle Ben got a promotion for getting us here. I've a good mind to put you all on report and let him take care of you! I don't think he'll have much patience with the likes of you when he gets back!"

The miscreants mumbled something about being sorry and that they wouldn't do it again.

"You're damn right you won't do it again! When I can't trust the rated men on this ship, then who the hell can I trust. You're supposed to set an example, a <u>good</u> example, is that clear?"

"Yes, sir," they all responded.

"All right. Now put those rifles and helmets away and help me get this barge back where it belongs before our new commander gets back and hangs you by the balls!"

Zale collected the gear to stow in the port locker. When he opened the hatch a young Filipino jumped out and said, "Please, sir, don't hang me by the balls. Me a guerilla." (He pronounced this word in the Spanish fashion.) "Me work for you. No trouble. My name Francisco."

"Well I'll be damned!" exclaimed the amazed ensign. "What the hell else can happen today? What am I supposed to do with <u>you</u>?"

"Please, sir, me work - cook, clean, sew. Me a guerilla."

"A what?" asked the ensign.

"Me fight Jops in hills. Me kill many Jops. Me good American."

"That's right," said Essex the reader. "These people <u>are</u> Americans of a sort."

"Sure," added the bosun. "There's plenty of them in the Fleet. They're stewards and stuff like that in the Officers'Mess. Hey, that would be pretty classy, sir, to have your own steward."

"Yeah," said Smyth as he warmed to the idea, "and he'd be handy to have around to deal with these people. Okay, we'll try it. Give him a cot under the tarp. He can start by helping the cook. But first we'll have to change his name to Frankie. Francisco is too much. Okay, Frankie?"

"Okay, sir. I be Frankie to stay on this ship."

"You be crazy to stay on this ship," said Berger.

The ensign led Frankie away to introduce him to the rest of the crew.

"Well come on you guys," said the bosun to his inanimate charges, "let's get to work. I wonder who's got the wheel?"

Seaman Dugan had the wheel, and he was doing a good job of steering the 166. The bosun let him keep it. "Okay," he said, "let's see if you can put us alongside one of them Ts out there without sinkin' us."

"What side to?' yelled Dugan from within the wheel house.

"Which ever one is easiest for you," replied the bosun, "just see to it that you don't scrape any of our rust off. That's the only thing holdin' this bucket together."

The bosun stood by to supervise his gang in securing the 166 to one of its sisters. The men didn't need any supervising, but what the hell. Soon they were snug alongside the 184.

The four adventurers hit the sack and were soon asleep. The remainder of the crew (with the exception of the gun-watch) also yielded to the afternoon heat. Soon all was quiet on the 166.

October 28

At 0150 on the morning of the 28th LTCMDRs Baxter and Bell had returned to the bay with their ships heavy with the heroic survivors of Taffy 3. Flares to eastward proclaimed their return.

Their shipmates had been anxiously awaiting that moment for 53 hours. They were quietly sipping their beer during their last few hours of waiting and watching. They went beserk when the blinkerlight proclaimed their return. Gone was the tension, the anxiety, and the melancholy. Out came the sequestered bottles of whiskey and beer. The delayed celebration could finally begin now that the group was together again. The serious drinking began. The old songs began to be sung again. Precious wind-up phonographs made their appearance along with equally treasured V-Discs. The soft tropic night suddenly erupted with jazz, vigorous voices, laughter and life. It was suddenly good to be young and alive again.

After a while the party attracted several other vessels. These were outrigger canoes called "bancas." Each of these had a man in the bow with a paddle, a man in the stern with a paddle, and a woman in the middle sitting on a mattress! When the

first "welcome wagon" came alongside, the bosun
yelled for Frankie.

"What the hell is <u>that</u>?" he asked as he
pointed at the appartition that had so suddenly and
quietly materialized from out the stygian gloom of
the bay.

"That is 'pom-pom' girl," explained Frankie.
"very good 'figgy-figgy'," he laughed.

"Figgy-figgy your ass! How much is it gonna
cost me?" asked the gallant bosun as he quickly
sized-up the situation.

Frankie spoke to the man in the stern, then he
spoke to the bosun. "Her father say six beers or six
packs of cigarettes. Is too much."

"Not to me, it ain't!" said the bosun as he
disappeared into the compartment only to promptly
re-appear with a case of suds on his shoulder. "<u>This</u>
oughtta last me a while," he laughed as he vaulted
over the four-foot high bulwark onto the catwalk.
He carefully placed the beer at the feet of the
stern-paddler who promptly opened one and tossed
another to his brother up forward. Then the bosun
walrussed himself onto the mattress and began to do
his version of the figgy-figgy. But before things
really got interesting the banca discreetly slid off
into the darkness from whence it had come.
Another banca immediately took its place.

The word soon spread.

Boats kept coming and going; guys fell into the water; young laughter filled the night.

Eventually the banca-rowers grew arm weary and beery. They secured their boats to the side of the 166 and then they hoisted the girls and their mattresses over the bulwark and onto the tank deck. The men eagerly dragged the mattresses up forward into the semi-darkness of the bow section. Six young women were soon in business. An hour later there weren't any more contributions to be made to the local economy, but that didn't stop the action. The girls and their relatives had been drinking just as much as had the men. By sunrise everyone was blotto, bloated, and blasted. Regardless, with the coming of the sun the natives departed with their loot and their mattresses. Ensign Smyth waved goodbye to them from his vantage point on the bridge. Then he collapsed into the beach chair. He smiled as he slept.

Along about mid-afternoon a few of the men began to stir in the compartment. Then the stories began, stories that were the mainstay of their conversation for months to come. Stories that are still being told. However, most good conversation requires drink to lubricate the larynx, to promote the flow of rhetoric, and to inspire eloquence. It also needs smoke to emanate from the speaker's mouth and nose so as to impart a mystical quality to his pronouncements.   But neither alcohol nor tobacco was available to the desperate crew members of the 166 on that memorable   morning after .

Lookouts were posted to scan the horizon for tell-tale smudges of smoke from the stacks of approaching freighters.   Desperate stratagems were broached. Frankie was turned to for intelligence -

"How   much   do   cigarettes   cost   ashore, Frankie?"

"Dos pesos, one dollar a pack."

"Jesus!"

"How much is beer?"

"The same - dos pesos - one dollar a can."

"Jumpin' Jesus, we gotta get some money!"

"I've pissed away a fortune," moaned the bosun.

"I've smoked away a fortune," coughed the cook.

"What are we gonna do? - When's payday? - Who knows?"

"Well we've got a piss-pot fulla money comin' to us, " said Zale, "and I want some of it!"   The others heartily agreed with his sentiments.

"I'll signal the 34 and try to find out when we're supposed to get paid in this outfit."

The encouragement of the crew was ringing in his ears as he climbed to the bridge.   He had to step over the snoring ensign to get to the blinker-light.

No one was awake on the 34 to acknowledge his signal. But while he was up there he noticed a freighter making a tentative approach to the bay.

"All hands on deck!" he yelled. The ensign stirred. "Man your sea details," continued Essex. "Cast off! Haul ass!" The proper order for getting underway had escaped him in that moment of excitement. The ensign was in no condition to help.

The men poured out of the compartment to see the cause of the excitement off to starboard. The 166 got underway in record time. Ensign Smyth finally woke up.

"Wha's goin' on?" he mumbled.

"There's a freighter off to starboard sir. I thought that she might be needing assistance."

"Yes, quite right, Essex. Good thinking. I'm going below. Let me know when we're through off-loading."

"Yes, sir," said Essex as he assisted Smyth in his descent of the ladder to the wheel house deck.

The 166 stalked the freighter until it dropped anchor, and then promptly went alongside. There was not any argument that time about whose lines would be used. They came snaking down as soon as the T was in position. Cargo nets soon followed. The first nets were filled with crates and boxes of ammunition. That particular Liberty ship did not turn out to be a cornucopia of "goodies." In fact, all that it provided the men was a raging thirst after muscling 180 tons of ammo boxes, etc. It only took an hour to deposit that amount of tonnage on the tank deck. During that interval several other Ts had been drawn to the freighter with equally high hopes. The ship could accommodate two of them on each side. Her cargo was off-loaded in record time. It turned out that she carried nothing but ammunition! Gloom pervaded the flotilla. But the men on the freighter were happy as hell to get out of there so quickly. Nothing so gladdens the heart of a seaman on an ammunition ship as does a fast turn-around in a war zone. She was out of the bay by sundown.

The 166 pointed her bow toward the beach. Her slow pace reflected her funereal mood. There was always something funereal about an LCT, but that day it was especially strong.

There was plenty of parking space on the beach. All of the LSTs had gone elsewhere. In fact, the 166 was the only vessel on the whole damn beach. Therefore her arrival had not gone un-noticed. An army staff car was soon roaring down the beach toward her. The car was followed by a truck. They both stopped in front of the ramp. A colonel stepped out of the car. He waved to them on the bridge. They waved back. The colonel yelled, "I want to talk to your commanding officer."

"Okay," replied Frisch, "just a minute." He scooted down below to roust the CO out of his rack. "There's an army officer on the ramp who wants to talk to you."

"What did you do this time?" roared the incensed commanding officer.

"Nothin'. Honest to God. We didn't do nothin'."

"If you guys stole any more scotch . . ."

"No, we didn't steal nothin'. What was there to steal?"

"Well we'll soon see." Smyth was hard put to find enough pieces to make a complete uniform, but he did well enough to make himself presentable under those conditions.

When he stepped out of the compartment he faced a mountain of boxes and crates. He had to crab his way over this obstacle to get to the ramp. He was not in any mood for an argument when he finally got there.   However, the officer waiting for him was not at all hostile. In fact, he shook hands with our dishevelled friend in a most cordial manner. The ensign was dumb-struck.

"The General was watching you this afternoon when you were off-loading that ship. He was most gratified by your industry, your efficiency, and your all-around excellence.   In recognition of your performance he has sent you some tokens of his appreciation." With that he turned to the soldiers in the truck and signalled them to unload it. Off came several cases of beer, a case of cigarettes, a great wheel of cheese, a giant bologna, and a crate of chickens.

When the men on the bridge saw what was happening they let out a "whoop", jumped off the bridge, and scrambled over the ammo with amazing facility. Soon each man in the crew was carrying a burden of joy back to the compartment.

Ensign Smyth thanked the officer and the General profusely. He invited the officer aboard, but he deferred. "Some other time," he said as he stepped back into his staff car. He roared off into the dusk back to his world of rank and privilege; a world that had opened for a moment and then had closed. Reality was that the 166 was once again a viable floating organism in the vast holding-tank of the U.S.N.

"I can't believe it," the men yelled once they were back in the compartment. "Look at all them goodies. Who'd a thunk it possible, I ask ya?"

"This only proves the ancient adage that virtue is its own reward," said a slightly confused Ensign Smyth.

"Yeah," interpreted the bosun, "heat up the stove,Cookie. Let's have baloney steaks for openers."

The baloney was the size and shape of an 8" shell.   Inch-thick steaks were cut off it and were then plopped onto frying pans - one to a pan. Wedges of cheese were cut from the wheel with sharp Kabars. Each wedge was the size and shape of a piece of lemon meringue pie.   The cheese was washed down with warm beer. Cigarette smoke once again filled the compartment.   A Christmas Eve atmosphere prevailed, and the General was Santa Claus. As the bosun said, beaming, with a mouth full of baloney and beer, "Who'd a thunk it?"

Indeed, who would have?

"And tomorrow," said the ensign, "we'll paint an 'E for Excellence' on the side of the wheel house, that'll show 'em!"

"Fuckin' A!" responded the men in a shout of joy.

End of Part I

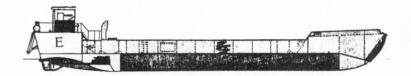

Part II

"For the duration plus . . ."

Being an account of how some of the men who were stuck overseas at the end of the war managed to survive that period of compulsory servitude, etc.

Chapter 12

The Post-Bellum Blues

1944 ended with war and rumors of more. Bell's group of landing craft was split-up and dispatched to various ports that were scheduled for invasion and occupation.   The ships of the Seventh Amphibious Force made 14 landings in the Philippines in a period of 44 days.

On the fifth of July General MacArthur officially announced the termination of hostilities in the Philippines.

The invasion of Japan was scheduled for the first of November.

Estimated American casualties - one million.

Estimated Japanese casualties - several millions.

On 6 August 1945 an atomic bomb was dropped on Hiroshima. The death toll amounted to 80,000.

On 9 August an atomic bomb was dropped on the oldest Christian city in the Orient - Nagasaki. The dead amounted to 35,000.

The war ended five days later.

You will not find any feelings of guilt among the men who were scheduled to invade Japan in regard to the use of atomic bombs to end the war.

Documents captured after the war revealed that their planned defense of the home islands was to rely on the use of Kamikazes to prevent the Americans from getting ashore. They had put 10,000 planes aside for this purpose; however, this time they were not going to concentrate on the carriers and other warships as they had done at Okinawa. This time they were going to go after the <u>landing craft</u> as they approached the beaches. They were willing to exchange one plane and one pilot for one landing craft loaded with men and equipment. They were not going to allow a single landing craft of <u>any</u> size to land a single American on their sacred soil if they could prevent it. And with those tactics they could have prevented it. The final battle was to be fought within a mile of their shoreline. The sea would have turned incarnadine. Possibly every landing craft in MacArthur's navy would have been wiped out. And the few surviving soldiers and marines that did manage to crawl ashore would have been met by 35 million soldiers and civilians eager to die for their emperor. No, there are no feelings of guilt among the men who were scheduled to invade Japan. Instead, there was a great sigh of relief.

The end of the war found LCT 166 and nine other Ts on Batangas Bay, 70 miles due south of Manila. The town of Batangas had become a "receiving ship" for thousands of GIs who had suddenly been declared surplus property.

All combatant ships suddenly found them
selves to be un-needed except as a means of
transportation for the equally un-needed combat
troops. It was a very strange turn-around. LCTs
suddenly became more important than battleships.
Who needs a battleship in peacetime? But the Ts
could still perform a useful service by moving men
and materiel.   Therefore, the crews of LCTs and
other "service ships" were the   last ones to be
discharged from the wartime navy.

Gloom once again pervaded the 166. Everyone
apparently was going home but they. Indeed, they
went ashore every night to witness some violent
"going home" parties.   They had plenty of money,
beer, booze, butts, and pom-pom girls - everything
that they had dreamed of when they were in
Hollandia.   They had everything except a ticket
home; therefore, they had nothing.

With the ending of hostilities, military service
suddenly became overwhelmingly unbearable to
millions of non-career servicemen.   When the war
ended so did their reason for being in the service, for
being overseas, for tolerating every tedious day away
from their homes and their people.   With the
exception of those who were sent to Japan for
occupation duty, there was little justification for
retaining any military or naval personnel in the far
reaches of the Pacific.   Yet many were retained

beyond the promised "duration plus six months."
Prisoners-of-war got home before they did. But
eventually the nightmare of frustration ended. Most
of the men got back to their homes; but a few of
them were sent to the prisons in Manila (Bilibid and
Santo Tomas) for a few years for assorted crimes
such as selling government property on the black
market. A few others were quietly hanged for
murder in the cellars of Santo Tomas (a former
university and prison camp for Americans). Others
were killed in a variety of accidents, shootings,
stabbings, and drownings. A few went blind and/or
crazy from drinking too much "tuba" or whatever
came to hand. A psychologist might have called it a
"difficult period of adjustment."

General MacArthur had declared the
Philippines secured in July. The following month the
war ended. At that point in time Luzon contained a
significant portion of the army and navy that Mac
had planned to use in his called-off invasion. These
were the hardbitten men that had fought their way
north from Guadalcanal, through the Solomon
Islands, through the Bismarck Archipelago, along
the coast of New Guinea, and finally through the
Philippines. They were the veterans of three years
of encounters with a most persistent and tenacious
enemy. They were not intimidated by the thought of
one more inning with the Jap, even if it were to be

played in <u>his</u> ball park.   But then suddenly it was over!   The enemy was disarmed, imprisoned for brief periods of time, and then sent home. The Americans were not dis-armed, they were suddenly "free", and there was nothing for most of them to do except to count up their "points" and wait for transportation back to the States.

On 15 August (VJ-Day) there were app. one and-a-half million American soldiers and 250,000 sailors on Luzon ready to stage for Japan.   The next day they were ready to stage for home.   They suddenly found themselves with time on their hands, money in their pockets, and a great thirst for whatever the islands had to offer.   Filipino entrepreneurs were not blind to the profit-making potential that the post-war months presented to them.   All of the bombed, blasted, and burned cities from Baguio to   Batangas to Tacloban rose from their liberated ashes to meet the needs of their wild young guests.   Primitive   night   clubs,   bars, restaurants, barber shops, and brothels bloomed in an orgy of profit-taking.

The Wild West was re-born overnight.   Luzon, in particular was the last frontier.   The visitors drank themselves into insensibility,   gambled with sublime   magnanimity,   fought   with   professional ferocity, and whored incessantly. (VD became such a problem in Manila that   MacArthur considered putting the town   off-limits, but he then decided against it.)

The MPs and SPs could not handle all of the action. The stockades and brigs were filled to over-flowing with happy incorrigibles. Courts-martial, unfortunately, were in constant session. But every night was still filled with the sounds of fights, riots, shootings, screams, fires, and a multitude of lesser outrages.   It was a group therapy session without equal. It was post-war Luzon.

More Americans died in Batangas after the war than were killed while the 11th Airborne Division was taking the place from the enemy. The post-war casualties were buried next to those that had been killed-in-action.   Their families were notified that they had died-in-the- line-of-duty. Regardless, they were all equally dead and were all considered to be equally heroic.

Among the living that August of 1945 were the officer and men of LCT 166.   Their morale was pretty dead, but that was something from which they would recover.   Spirits were especially low among the older members of the crew - Jazinski, Essex, Zale, Berger, and Evans.   They all had enough points to go home, but unfortunately for them they were crew on a vessel that still had a job to do.   The other half of the crew - Sidney, Frisch, Dugan, Pacelli, and Temple were resigned to putting in another six-months before they would be eligible for discharge.   Ensign Smyth was also in the latter category, but he had the advantage of a liberal arts education that gave him a philosophical perspective denied to lesser mortals. His philosophy could be summed-up in one word - "SHIT!"

VJ-Day plus one found the 166 abandoned on the beach at Batangas. The entire crew was still ashore recovering from the previous day's and night's festivities. The other Ts in the group were in an equal state of abandonment. They were all docilely scraping against one another as the tide rose and fell. The only witness to that desolate scene on that sunny morning was a Seaman First Class by the name of Hank Johnson.

Seaman Johnson had been pursuing the elusive 166 all over the Southwest Pacific. His orders were quite specific, but no one really seemed to know where the 166 was at any given moment. As a result of this confusion, Johnson found himself aboard a series of LCIs and LSTs bound for various ports in New Guinea, the Admiralty Islands, and the Philippines. This fruitless quest lasted for two months. It finally ended on August 16 as described above.

Seaman Johnson stood on the lonely beach looking at the row of abandoned LCTs wondering what the hell had been so urgent about his reporting to this forsaken group. He sat down on the sand next to his seabag and contemplated his fate.

Johnson was 19 years old, tall, thin, and disconsolate. He had joined the Navy soon after he had graduated from high school in June of 1944. He had gone through nine weeks of boot camp, five months of Gunner's Mates schools, one month on a troop ship, two months in pursuit of the 166, and now there he was sitting on the beach, the war over, and the whole goddam place was deserted! What a useless waste of time, he thought to himself. He didn't realize at that time that he was one of the many that had been sent over to participate in the invasion of Japan. The atomic bomb had saved his life. Now all that he had to do was to hold onto it.

His reverie was interrupted by the sudden appearance of Tom Essex. Tom's materialization was rather startling in that his entire uniform consisted of a pair of GI shorts. In addition to being almost naked, he was bloody, bruised, and amused at something beyond the ken of the stunned Johnson. He was even more stunned when he saw Essex stumble aboard the 166 - his ship! He didn't know what to do other than watch Essex stagger about the tank deck in a state of sublime euphoria. Finally he collapsed on a cot under the tarp. His laughter was soon replaced by snores.

Johnson picked up his seabag and cautiously followed Essex's track aboard the 166. He peeked inside the chaotic mess called the crews' quarters and decided not to go in.   Instead he sat down on one of the cots laid out under the tarp. Listening to Essex snore soon became a bore. Also, his stomach was growling.   He decided to enter the compartment in hopes of finding something edible therein.   Upon opening the refrigerator he found a can of beer, a wedge of cheese, a hunk of bologna, and a can of condensed milk.   He looked about for some bread or crackers to eat with the cheese and bologna.   He found a case of C-rations which he opened for the crackers contained therein. He also found other canned items that were palatable.   Thus he ate his first meal aboard the 166.   He finished his brunch while sitting on a cot near the unconscious Essex. Suddenly the generator began to gasp for gas. Johnson didn't know what to do in such a situation. He stared at the thing until it uttered its final sputter and died.

"That's all right," said a voice from above. "I come down and fix it."

A dark brown leg appeared on the ladder leading down to the tank deck. Johnson didn't know which way to jump. The brown leg was followed by the brown remainder of Frankie.

"Hello. My name Francisco, but they call me Frankie. I from Tacloban. I messboy this ship. What your name?"

"Johnson, Hank Johnson."

"You be crew this ship?" asked Frankie as he looked at Johnson's seabag.

"Yeah, I guess so," answered the disconsolate Johnson.

"Oh is not so bad. Plenty liberty. Plenty tuba. Plenty figgy-figgy. You have good time this ship."

"Where is everybody?   Who's that?" he asked pointing at the inert Tom Essex.

"That Essex.   He signalman.   Damn good man. Plenty tuba.   Plenty figgy-figgy," he laughed.

"Where is everybody?"

"They all go big party for end of war. They all get plenty drunk, plenty fucked-up. I don't know where they are now. Maybe in brig. Who knows? Excuse me now. I have to put more gas in engine or else ice-box get warm and all hell break loose."

"How long have you been on this barge?" Johnson asked while Frankie was ministering to the generator.

"Since October."

"October?   In Tacloban?   You mean that this bucket was in the Battle of Leyte Gulf?"

"Sure.   This bucket been all over the fucking place.   Is full of holes from Jop bastards shooting it. This some old bucket!" he said proudly.

"Well how come you're up here if your home's in Tacloban?"

"How come you here if your home in America?"

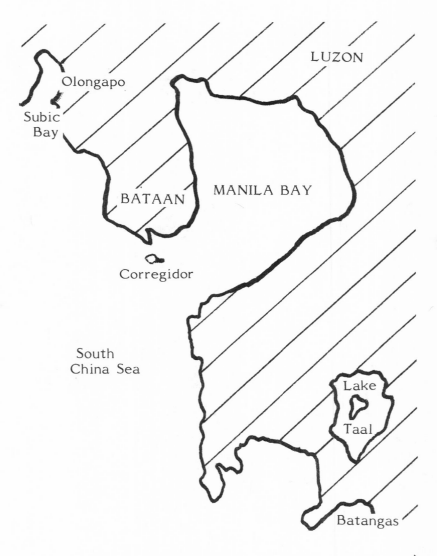

(This map is not to be used for navigational purposes.)

" 'cause I'm in the Navy, that's how come."

"Well I'm in Navy, too.   Me Messboy First Class. I shit you not."

"Where did you learn to speak English," asked the amused Johnson.

"I learn in school before war. But the Sisters taught us a funny kind of English - not like we talk in Navy."

"How many men are on this ship?"

"Three. You, me, and Essex."

"I mean how many are in the crew?"

"Twelve. You make thirteen! Oh Holy Mary save us! You number thirteen!"

"No I'm not.   I'm number twelve. You're number thirteen. I'm supposed to be here, you're not!"

"No, is too many. Is bad. Somebody sure get killed now."

"How can anybody get killed?" asked the naive Johnson. "The war's over."

"They get killed all time around here. This place more fucked-up than Tacloban. That's why I stay in wheel house. Is safe in there. No holes in wheel house."

"Well you're not alone now.   Do you know where I'm supposed to sleep? Do I get a locker?"

"You sleep out here. No room inside. No locker inside either until somebody get killed. Then you go inside."

"Stop talking about someone getting killed. No one's gonna get killed. I'd rather sleep out here anyway."

"You don't mind generator?"

"I don't mind anything."

"Good, you won't get anything."

"I didn't get much for breakfast. There doesn't seem to be much aboard in the line of food. How do you feed 'em?"

"I don't feed 'em. The cook feeds 'em. I just clean up."

"But where do they get their food?"

"Army truck bring food now and then. Sometime we get food from Navy. Most time we steal food from big ships. We better get back to work plenty quick or we starve to death. Everything all fucked-up plenty bad."

"What do you mean, 'get back to work'."

"We unload those big ships," Frankie said as he pointed to the freighters within the wide sweep of the bay. "They loaded with food, and Chestefields, and Schlitz. We don't need no fucking army or navy to feed us. We take care ourselves. But we better get back to work plenty quick or we starve to death. I shit you not."

At that moment there suddenly appeared on the ramp a trimen of seamen consisting of Dugan, Frisch, and Pacelli. Frisch was in the middle. He was the biggest of the three, so he had the supporting role. Dugan was wearing a white hat, GI shorts, and combat boots. Frisch was wearing a straw hat and a denim shirt. Pacelli was wearing a T-shirt and a pair of dungarees that were too big for him. If the three of them had pooled their garments they could have come up with one complete outfit. However, they were completely oblivious to their unorthodox appearance. They were totally absorbed in the words and music of a few songs that were popular in that time and place. Some of you may remember such old favorites as, "Fuck 'em All", "No Balls at All", and "She had Freckles on Her, But She Was Nice". Well anyway, they were earnestly trying to do justice to those ditties. They must have been very drunk because they were very serious. Pacelli was losing patience with the other two.

"What'sa matter with you guys?" he burped. "Can'tcha remember nothin'? I been teachin' ya all these songs and ya can't remember nothin'. I never seen such dummies. Where's my boots? Somebody took my boots! Dugan took my boots!

"I didn't take ya stupid boots! These are Frisch's boots!"

"How come you're wearin' my boots?" asked the barefoot Frisch. "I ain't got no boots!"

" 'cause ya traded me for my shirt. Otherwise you woulda been balls-ass naked. Then the MPs would have picked you up. Is that what you want, ya dumb

Dutch dope?"

"Don't call me a dope.   I"m a high school graduate, I am.   That's more than you are, you dumb Irish idiot."

Frisch and Pacelli thought that that was very funny.   They laughed so hard that Frisch fell down. When he fell they all fell.   That was even funnier to them than the original remark.   They laughed until the gasped.   Then they started to crawl the length of the hot tank deck toward the shade provided by the tarpaulin.

There were three cots left for them to occupy.   Soon they were all asleep.   Their combined snores almost drowned out the generator. Essex, Dugan, Frisch, Pacelli, and the generator - the quintet from Los Borrachones by Bacchus.

"Are they all like this?" Johnson asked.

"Oh no," replied Frankie,"these are the good guys.   Wait till you see the bosun, and Zale, and the cook, and Berger!.   You gotta look out for Berger. He's a mean bastard when he's drunk, and he's drunk most of the time."

"What's the captain like?"

"Ensign Smyth?   Oh he's okay.   He should be back soon.   He drinks alla time, but he hardly ever get drunk.   Not like others.   He okay-Joe."

Ensign Smyth arrived on cue.   He drove aboard in a jeep that he had commandeered somewhere in the night.   There was a body in the back seat. Frankie and Johnson ran to give the ensign a hand. They lifted the inert form of the bosun and carried him into the compartment where they put him in his rack. Then they ran back to the jeep. Ensign Smyth was frantically digging in one of the forward lockers looking for an old tarp. He pulled it out of the locker, and then the three of them put it over the jeep. Once it was completely covered, the ensign breathed a sigh of relief.

"Jesus," he sighed, "that was some trip!"

"Where you find jeep?" asked Frankie.

"I found it abandoned in front of the Officers' Club. I decided to give it a good home. Wow, I had some ride through town. Everybody tried to stop me. Somebody even took a shot at me. I think it was an MP. I didn't stop until I saw 'Boats' standing in the middle of the road takin' a piss. I got him in the back seat and then hauled ass. Man, is that place crazy. There's bodies passed out all over . Wow! Rosie's saloon got burned to the ground. I saw a naked broad runnin' through town with a platoon of GIs after her. There were three fights in the Club. Jesus, what a night! Is everybody aboard?"

"Only what you see and hear."

"Who's this?" he asked.

"This Hank Johnson," replied Frankie. "He just come aboard."

"Visiting?"

"No, sir," replied Johnson.   "I've been assigned to this vessel."

"God help you," replied the ensign. "What's your rate?"

"Seaman First, Gunner's Mate Striker, sir."

"Jesus, just what we need - another gunner's mate.   The fuckin' war's over, so they send me a gunner's mate striker! What I need is a motor mac that's got his head on straight, but they send me a gun-mechanic instead!   Well at least you can replace Zale. We sure as hell don't need two of you aboard.

Frankie was relieved that Zale was going to be replaced.   That would reduce their number to twelve without anyone getting killed.

"Yes, sir," replied Johnson for want of anything better to say.

"Yes, sir," muttered Smyth, "yes, sir. Jesus! I'm gonna lie down. Don't nobody disturb me unless is something very important.   And leave that jeep alone.   If someone comes lookin' for it, you don't know nothin'. Let me handle it, savvy?"

"Yes, sir," they both answered.

"Good. Now get outta my way for I'm bound for the Rio Grande."

"What he mean by that?" Frankie asked as they watched the ensign weave toward the compartment.

"I don't know. Maybe he's from Texas."

"No, he ain't from Texas.   He hate Texas.

He hate that fucking song - The Stars at Night are Big and Bright - he say he kill the next one who sing that song on his ship.   He got big temper sometime, but he good Joe anyway.   Let's go on bridge.   Is better up there."

After they were seated atop the wheel house, Johnson asked, "How long has the ensign been on this barge?"

"I don't know.   He come up from New Guinea on this barge.   They <u>all</u> come up from New Guinea. The bosun he come up from   Australia.   They <u>some</u> salty bastards, I shit you not."

"How many ships are there in this group?"

"I don't know.   Count 'em. They're all here on the beach.   You got more goddam   questions than MPs.   What else you want to know?"

"Who's that coming down the beach?"

The object of their attention was motor-mac Berger.   He was alone.   He looked as though he had spent the night in a rice paddy.   He was mud from head to toe, and that   was all that he was wearing except for his skivvies. He went aboard the adjoining T thinking that it was the 166.   Upon realizing his mistake he climbed over the bulwark, attempted to jump the gap separating the two vessels, fell into the space between, and rose cleansed if not chastened. When he finally got onto the   right vessel he was in no mood for any more impromptus. Upon seeing that all of the cots were occupied, he tipped Essex's cot until the recumbent figure rolled heavily onto the steel deck. Essex awoke with a roar. The two of them tore into each other for about ten minutes until Berger's extra weight forced his opponent's back on to the deck. Berger then sat on the signalman's chest, then he methodically set about to rearrange his adversary's facial features. Berger would have killed Essex if he had been allowed to continue his undertaking without interruption. But the fight had awakened everyone but the bosun. Berger was lucky that the bosun was unconscious because he would have killed the motor-mac if he had seen what was happening to his friend. The other crew members managed to separate the two combatants. Smyth put Essex in the jeep and drove him to the hospital. He returned with an armed SP to arrest Berger. The two of them took the now-chastened MM to the brig. The official brig was so crowded that the overflow was herded into an enclosure made of chicken wire. There the miscreants sat on the shadeless ground under the observation of several armed marines who enjoyed their work. Berger suddenly became penitent, but he did not return to the 166. He spent some time in a psychiatric hospital in Manila, and was then shipped home. That left eleven men on the 166's roster. Fireman Temple would be promoted to fill Berger's place in the engine room. The engines would never notice the difference.

Ensign Smyth returned with the SP acting as chauffeur.   The ensign was driven up to the ramp, he got out, and then the jeep drove off with the SP still at the wheel.   That was the last that he ever saw of that jeep.   The authorities had informally decided not to prosecute him if he promised not to steal any more jeeps.   He promised.   The sight of that chicken-wire enclosure would prompt anyone to promise anything.   Our ensign had to settle for a boat.

The boat came into view that night under the command of the cook.   It was a row-boat of about eight feet in length which Evers had commandeered somewhere along the rim of the bay.   He secured it to the stern anchor-guard before climbing aboard. Ensign Smyth was much taken with the boat.   All that it needed was an outboard motor . . .

"Where the hell are we going to get an outboard motor?" asked the ensign the next morning of the survivors that had gathered for breakfast.

"Where the hell are we going to get some food?' asked Evers.   "There's nothin' left but C-rations."

'To hell with it," said Smyth.   "Let's go eat at Quino's."

"Now you're talkin'," said the bosun.

"But first you guys have got to clean up,

shave, and put on a decent uniform."

"But we don't have any decent uniforms."

"Then open some of those cases of trade goods that you've got. This is an emergency."

One of the cases contained officers' khakis. There were enough for each man to be outfitted in a shiny new uniform. They didn't all fit perfectly, but what the hell. Smyth led his contingent of what looked like seven boot-ensigns off the T, up the beach, and into town to Quino's for ham and eggs.

In those days the town of Batangas was similar to the town of Tacloban - blasted and burned buildings in various stages of reconstruction; hordes of half-dressed children playing in the dirt roads; ragged old men lounging in the sun; dozens of small family businesses trying to eke out a living, and dozens of saloons catering to the needs of the latest occupation force. Reconstruction was progressing at a rapid rate, but, as in Tacloban, the primary building materials were bamboo, thatch, and whatever they could salvage from damaged buildings or scrounged from the army. They did a remarkable job with the little that they had to work with.

Military vehicles dominated the transportation scene. Mobility for the natives was provided in the form of taxis called "calesas" which were high, two-wheeled pony carts. They could accommodate two Filipinos plus the driver, or one American plus the driver.   More than one American on board would usually cause the cart to tip rearward thus lifting the pony off the ground.   Freight hauling for civilians was provided by cumbersome two-wheeled wagons pulled by water buffalo.

Quino's Bar and Restaurant was very similar to Vargas' establishment in Tacloban. It too was a long, narrow building divided into three sections - the bar in front, the kitchen and tables in the middle, and a private room in the rear with a garden view.   The major difference between the two structures was an additional story topside.   Senor Quino and his family lived upstairs.   He also had an additional room up there for occasional paying guests and/or emergencies.

Quino's place catered to naval personnel, especially LCTmen.   There were about 100 of the latter in Batangas.   They comprised a coterie on which the proprietor could depend.   Other military personnel would occasionally wander in, but they had other places which they could call their own.   Thus were the territorial   imperatives established in the town of Batangas.

Quino welcomed Ensign Smyth and his seven shiny shipmates. (Frankie remained on board to keep an eye on things, otherwise the T would have been stripped clean.)   Quino prepared a monumental breakfast for his loyal patrons. They cleaned out his larder. He had to send out for more food. When it came time to pay the check they discovered that no one had any money!

"Is all right," said Senor Quino. "You pay me when your ship come in," he laughed. It was a cliché, but it was very apt. It was time for them to get back to work. They thanked their host and were about to leave when he asked, "Don't you want the other two guys?"

"What other two guys?"

"Zale and Temple. They've been here long enough."

"Where are they?"

"Topside. Come, I show you."

Quino led them upstairs to his special accommodations for paying guests and/or emergencies. Zale and Temple were definitely in the latter category. Zale was sleeping on the floor. Temple was stretched diagonally across the big double bed. They were carried below, out into the street, dumped into a wagon, and slowly returned to the 166. Ensign Smyth led the procession. An honor guard of shiny seamen walked on either side of the conveyance. Giggling kids fell in behind. Port bound traffic was delayed for an hour while waiting for the water buffalo to shift gears. The only crewman still missing was Sidney.

The next few days were devoted to unloading freighters in order for the Ts to replenish their stock of trade goods. The men took just enough to provide them with their basic needs - food, beer, smokes, and Liberty money (they still were not getting paid). Beer was worth 20 pesos (10 dollars) a case on the blackmarket. Food was kept aboard except for canned fish after which the natives lusted. Cigarettes had a minimal value on the market.
Clothing brought the top peso. A fortune in goods was transported from the ships to the shore. Opportunities appeared for getting rich (by GI standards), but very few of the men took advantage of their position. Some of those that did spent a few years behind the walls of Bilibid and Santo Tomas prisons.

Ensign Smyth received permission from the interim "group commander" aboard the 182 (LTJG Jameson) to transfer the surplus GM Zale to Olongapo, Subic Bay, for re-assignment or shipment home. The only problem was that Olongapo was 120 miles northwest of Batangas by truck or buffalo-cart. Neither was a dependable means of getting to Subic Bay. Smyth suggested that the 166 deliver Zale to his destination. Surprisingly, Jameson acquiesced to this suggestion. He also surprised Smyth by saying that the 182 would accomapny him on his journey. (As you know, LCTs never travelled

alone for any distance greater than a nautical mile.)
Apparently Lieutenant Jameson needed a change, so
he and his crew were going along for the ride.

At a speed of five knots the 120 mile voyage
would take 24 hours (if all went well). Officers
Jameson and Smyth saw no reason for such haste.
They decided to be underway only during daylight
hours.   Such reckoning would put them in the
vicinity of Corregidor by sundown.   They planned to
spend that night in Mariveles Harbor across from the
island. Everyone was pleased with this arrangement.

On the morning of 1 September 1945 the two
LCTs pointed their blunt bows into the Verde Island
Passage for the voyage north. It was their first
peacetime journey. Pacelli relaxed. A holiday air
prevailed among the survivors of one of the most
unbelievable voyages of the war. Another was about
to begin, but this one would be more unforgettable
than unbelieveable.

Chapter 13

On the way to Subic Bay
Where the flyin' fishes play.

Upon clearing the Verde Island Passage they entered the South China Sea. It looked like any other body of water upon which they had sailed. The major difference lay in the fact that that body of water did not contain or support any man-made threats to their existence. They were finally freed from that anxiety. It was a marvelous moment. However, their reverie was soon shattered by the sound of an M-1 being fired. Ensign Smyth had decided to do some target shooting. The targets were flying fish. Every round fired into those waters produced any number of fish which would skitter along the pale green surface for distances of up to 100 feet. They were very challenging targets. Few, if any of them got hit, but they certainly provided some exotic shooting.

Each T had several rifles aboard. There were also several cases of surplus ammunition. Soon every rifle on both Ts were blasting away at the elusive targets. The firing continued for several hours until everyone had his turn and eventually became bored with it. By then it was beginning to be late in the afternoon. They were approaching the entrance to Manila Bay.

"Jesus, Manila Bay at last!" exclaimed the bosun who was at the wheel. "We finally made it!

Let's go in!"

"No," replied Ensign Smyth. "Our destination is Mariveles tonight, and Olongapo tomorrow. Maybe we can visit Manila tomorrow, I don't know. I'll have to talk it over with Jameson. He's the boss."

"Jesus," repeated the bosun. "Just think of it - liberty in Manila! I've sailed this bucket all the way from Australia to Manila! That calls for a celebration!"

"Well you'll just have to wait a little while longer for your celebration," said the ensign. "It's not in our plans for tonight."

"What was the best 'Liberty town' you was ever in, Boats?" asked Essex who was lounging in the wheel house.

"Here or in the States?"

"In the States?"

"Saint Louis was the best," he said without a moment's hesitation. "Detroit was good,too. And Chicago. All of them towns was great, but Saint Louis was the best."

"Why?"

" 'cause that's where they make the beer! And those German girls were real friendly. But best of all, there ain't many sailors in that part of the country; nor soldiers neither. Yeah, the MidWest is the place to be. To them a serviceman was somethin' special. Yeah, Saint Louis was somethin' else," he sighed.

"You're from that part of the country, ain'tcha?" asked Essex.

"Yeah, Detroit, the Hamtramck section where all us Polocks live."

"Ya goin' back there?"

"I guess so.   I'd rather go back to Brisbane, but I guess I'll end up in Detroit."

"Why dont you go back to Saint Louis?" asked the ensign from the other corner of the wheel house.

" 'cause it'll all be changed.   It won't be like it was durin' the war.   In war time we're all heroes. In peace time it's different."

"You can't go home again," said the literate Mister Smyth.

"Exactly," agreed the bemused bosun.

"Brisbane won't be the same after three years either," said Essex.

"Yeah, I guess you're right," sighed the bosun again.   "I might as well go back to Detroit. There's things there that don't change."

"Like what?"

"Like my family and friends, and the old neighborhood, and the old ways."

"Yeah," agreed Essex, "them things don't change much.   Ya gonna get married?"

"I am married, but I ain't heard from the bitch in two years.   I think I'll go home just to give her a good kick in the ass, and then maybe I'll ship over. There's worse ways to spend your life."

"Like what?"

"Like workin' on an assembly line. Like livin' in the same place all the time. Like gettin' fat, and bald, and lonesome. At least in the Navy I'm never lonesome. I don't always like all the ship's company, but I like most of 'em. Guys like Zale, ya know? I'm gonna miss him. But maybe he'll ship over, too, and then we'll see the rest of the world together. There's still a lot of places I ain't seen. And I don't know of any other way of gettin' to see 'em except from the deck of a ship. So I guess you're lookin' at a thirty-year man. After that I'll open a beer hall in Saint Louis and give free beers to old shipmates. You're all invited."

"Ya mean I'll have to wait twenty years for a free beer?"

"No, Tom, I'll buy ya one tomorrow in Manila. Ain't that right, Skipper?"

"We'll see. I'll talk it over with Jameson tonight. It's his decision, not mine."

"Okay", replied the bosun, "but it don't really matter that much. And anyway, we've got enough beer to have our own celebration, and it's all free."

"Don't you know that it's against Navy Rules and Regs to drink aboard a naval vessel?" joshed the ensign.

"Since when is this a naval vessel?" replied Essex. "I thought we belonged to MacArthur."

"That's right!" exclaimed Smyth. "Therefore the Rules and Regs don't apply to us," he smiled at his logic.

"Is this news to you?" asked Essex.

"No, but I thought I'd make it formal."

Down the voice-tube at that moment came the announcement, "I think I see Corregidor off the starboard bow."

"Who'm I talkin' to?" as the bosun.

"Dugan."

"Well get down here Dugan and take the wheel. I wanna get a look at that island."

"Well so do I," whined Dugan.

"Get your ass down here or I'll have your liver for lunch!"

Dugan responded immediately to the bosun's request. Then he and Smyth and Essex climbed the ladder to the bridge. They all wanted to see Corregidor.

There are few names that had as strong an emotional appeal to the people of that generation as did the name of Corregidor. It was there that MacArthur and Wainwright made their last stand. It was from there that MacArthur departed for Australia. It was there that Wainwright was finally forced to surrender what was left of the American army in the Philippines.   Corregidor was a bitter wound that healed slowly in the minds and hearts of the American people. It is one of the few names that are still remembered from the Pacific war. Corregidor, Guadalcanal, and Iwo Jima are about the only names that still live in the fading recesses of the minds of a fading generation. But during the 1940s Corregidor meant something special to Americans, so all hands were eager to take a good look at it.

There were about two hours of daylight left when they came abeam of Corregidor. The 182 signalled "Follow Me" on the blinker light and then headed for that deserted shore. Soon both Ts were abreast of each other on a narrow beach at the lower end of the island. All hands scurried ashore to explore the historic site.   All but the superstitious Frankie, that is.

Corregidor is shaped like a tadpole.   The massive head of the tadpole was called "Topside" by the marines who once occupied the ruined barracks on its heights. The tail half of the tadpole was called "Bottomside."   Thus it was an uphill climb for the intrepid tourists that day.

The place stank of death. Unburied skeletons were still to be seen in the bush. Japs were still manning the field guns which they had placed in open caves in anticipation of repelling invaders. Yes, they were still there, but they were very dead. Flamethrowers had fused them into their upright positions behind their guns. They still wore their blackened helmets atop their yellow skulls. Empty sockets looked seaward for the enemy. They grinned at the unarmed tourists who rushed by them in feverish pursuit of souvenirs.

The tourists climbed to the entrance to the famed Malinta Tunnel that had housed both American and Japanese defenders during their respective last days on the "Rock." An estimated 2,000 enemy soldiers had committed "seppuku" in that tunnel by blowing up their ammunition supply. It smelled like a mass grave that had not been covered over. The men soon lost their enthusiasm for souvenir hunting. There was nothing there but death and bones and rats and big red ants.

"Let's get the hell out of here!" yelled LT Jameson. No one objected. They all returned to their vessels, backed off the beach, and headed for Mariveles Harbor across the way. All that they took with them were some images that would far outlast any tangible reminders that they might have found during their tour of the "Rock."

Mariveles Harbor is located at the southern tip of the Bataan Peninsula. It too is a haunted place. It was there that the beaten Americans and their

Filipino allies had been marshalled to begin their infamous 90-mile Death March to prison camp John O'Donnell.   An estimated 10,000 prisoners of war died on that merciless trek.

That night in the harbor was also a depressing experience.   What had started out as a lark that morning had rapidly developed into something else.   They could feel the oppressive black bulk of Mount Bataan brooding behind them. The moon was down, thus plunging the whole area into funereal darkness.   A few lights winked from the town of Mariveles, like candles at a wake.   It wasn't much of a farewell party for Gunner Zale. The men drank their beer in silence, alone with their thoughts, and then went quietly to their bunks or cots.   The war was over, but its melancholy melody lingered on.   A few days later one of the men read in the Navy News (printed in Manila) that 20 enemy soldiers had given themselves up on Corregidor.

The tourists were eager to continue their tour elsewhere the following morning.   For the first time in memory there was not a single crewman who was suffering from a hangover. They were all bright-eyed and bushy-tailed, and keen to get the hell out of that weird area. By 0800 they were underway for the northwest side of the Bataan peninsula.

Subic Bay is the Pearl Harbor of the Philippines.   It is the most important American naval base in the Far East. Adjacent to the base is the city of Olongapo. This city is half navy and half civilian. The following message was painted on a large sign which used to be displayed at the side of the road which led from the base to the city:

DON'T GAMBLE WITH YOUR LIFE OR VISION.
LIQUOR IN THIS AREA HAS CAUSED DEATH
AND BLINDNESS.
MOST PROSTITUTES IN THIS AREA ARE
INFECTED.
BETTER BE SAFE THAN SORRY.

In addition to this public-service message, the Navy had built the biggest beer hall in the islands (perhaps the world) in an effort to keep the men on the base and away from the posted charms of Olongapo City. The effort was an unqualified success. Beer was selling for a dollar a can in the City. It was selling for a dime a can on the base. The whores and B-Girls of the City were still a powerful draw, but they only did a fraction of the business that they might have done but for the vigilance of our familial Navy.

As the two LCTs neared the Subic Bay anchorage they were challenged by a blinker- light from a signal tower which controlled the traffic on the Subic "road." The signalman on the 182 received instructions as to where they could anchor. The 166 tied alongside the 182. Then they hailed a boat to take them ashore.   However, <u>all</u> hands could not go ashore together that time because Subic Bay is NAVY and the   Rules and Regs had to be observed there. One officer had to remain aboard the two craft. That duty fell on Ensign Smyth.   One half of each crew also had to remain aboard.   On the 166 that duty fell on the younger half of the crew.   That was one of the rare times when rank and rate determined priorities on the Ts.

Zale said goodbye to the duty-bound group, and then he dropped his seabag into the bum-boat. The heavy canvas bag was followed by Zale, Essex, the cook, the bosun, and the gang from the 182. Once they got ashore the salty trio escorted Zale to the enlisted mens' barracks where they got him properly signed-in.   He was assigned a bare cot upon which he dropped his seabag.   Then the four of them went in search of the "biggest goddam beer hall in the world."   They were determined to diminish its stature to an appreciable degree.   But first they had to buy "beer chits" for ten cents each. Each chit was the size of a movie-ticket.   There was no limit on how many you could buy.   The average purchase measured out to app. one fathom in   length.   The men draped the tickets around their necks lei-style. The next step was to get on one of the several long lines that slowly snaked their way into the large Quonset Hut that dispensed the denary drafts.   Each man bought six cold cans, retired to one of the picnic tables that the navy had thoughtfully placed beneath the palm trees, and proceeded to "splice the main brace." It was a grand day for splicing - not too hot or humid with just enough breeze to blow the smoke away. They whiled away the afternoon with drinking beer, reminiscing, laughing, and standing in lines. Along about chow-time they generously escorted their friend to the mess hall. There they enjoyed a meal of fried pork chops, reconstituted potatoes, real gravy, canned vegetables, fresh bread, canned butter, canned applesauce, ice cream, fresh coffee, and a real apple. They hadn't seen an apple in months.

The lack of fresh food was a painful problem to the men who had been on small ships too long. Their restricted diets were raising hell with the digestive systems of men whose innards expected to encounter fresh food more often than once a quarter.

Our dyspeptic trio was back aboard the 166 by eight o'clock that night. Many black looks were directed at the tardy trio, but they couldn't have cared less. They had given their buddy a good send-off, and that was all that mattered to them.

The next morning the two Ts got underway for the return leg of their journey. LT Jameson had decided that it would be all right for them to visit Manila. What the hell, he thought, we've earned a vacation. And who knows when we'll get another chance to see the place?

So for the first time in their careers the Ts steered a course of south by east.

Manila Bay presented a panorama of ruin. An estimated 380 ships had sunk beneath its one-thousand square-mile surface. A forest of masts broke the surface from ships that had settled in the more shallow sections of the bay. There was so much steel on the bottom that it threw their compasses out of whack.

"Look at the fucking compass!" exclaimed Essex who was manning the wheel as they entered the bay. "It's doin' a goddam rhumba!"

"I ain't seen nothin' like that since Iron Bottom Bay down in Guadalcanal," responded the bosun as he studied the compass. "It's either a lot of ships down there or a lot of empties."

"We've sailed over a lot of empties before," replied Essex,"but I've never seena compass act like this before."

"Yeah, look at all them masts stickin' out of the water. This place is a fuckin' graveyard. A graveyard of ships - theirs and ours."

"Is this all they've got up here - dead ships and dead men?" asked the impressionable Essex.

"What's the matter?" asked the bosun. "You act like you've never seen it before."

"Not like <u>this</u>, I ain't.   And that stinkin' island! It's enough to make ya puke!"

"Well   brace   yourself,"   interjected   the omnipresent ensign as he looked through his binoculars. "That ruin ahead of us is what's left of the city of Manila. "

MacArthur had forbade the bombing of Manila in an effort to save his beloved "Pearl of the Orient" from excessive damage. He need not have bothered. The Japanese had put up their usual fight. The Americans had countered with equal determination. The result was that 1,200 Americans; 20,000 Japanese, and 100,000 Filipinos were killed in the battle for Manila. What artillery and fire had not destroyed, Japanese demolition charges had. The city was devastated.

The two Ts slowly picked their way between the wrecks in the bay until they were close enough to what had once been the Manila waterfront. The 182 did not turn off its engines nor drop its hook. Neither did the 166. All hands silently stared at the ruins as their engines idled. The lieutenant yelled from the bridge of the 182, "Does anyone still want to go ashore?" No one replied. "Then let's haul ass!" Both vessels slowly came about and headed away from the remains of the "Pearl" city.

Batangas didn't seem so bad to them once they had seen what the rest of Luzon was like. In fact, the thought of returning to Batangas was the best thing that had occurred to them since they had left that crazy place three long days before.

The weather rapidly deteriorated as they plodded south. The monsoon was sending its outriders across the South China Sea. Rain would be the featured event on the weather maps for the next three months. Rain-induced boredom would become the dominant characteristic of the men housed within the confines of the LCTs. There wasn't a helluva lot to do to break the boredom either. There weren't any books to read, and few magazines to stare at. Card games, but no gambling, some times broke the spell. Unloading ships was their major distraction, but even that became a bore.

Sleeping became an important part of each day's routine. When there was nothing else to do they would go ashore to drink at Quino's, listen to his radio and V-Discs, and get laid.

Getting laid was no problem as long as you had the ten-peso admission fee. There were several "pom-pom" girls set up within an easy walk of Quino's place. Their shacks were located behind the buildings on the main drag. It was customary for the men to visit one of the girls after he had been drinking for a few hours. It was a pleasant way to end an evening. It's a custom that is still observed throughout the civilized world.

Filipino women who chose to be pros did not have an easy time of it because they do not grow very big to the pound. Also, they were not terribly exciting to those young Americans whose fantasies at that time favored such types as Rita Hayworth, Betty Grable, and Lana Turner. But a "pom-pom" girl in the bush was worth more than a sex-pot on the mind.

Venereal disease was not a problem among the sailors stationed in Batangas even though prudent behavior is not a characteristic of drunken sailors. Their remarkable lack of VD was probably the result of them all subsidizing the same few women. Those whores were a select group. If they were ever seen fraternizing with other servicemen they were crossed off the list. So most of them remained loyal to the Navy. As a result, the women prospered and the men remained healthy. Whatever the reason, clap was not a problem among those sybarites of the western sea.

Drinking, however, <u>was</u> a problem. There was so much beer and tuba available that boozing became an accepted part of the daily routine after the war. This of course prompted somnolence which in turn promoted the passage of time. But this can be a perilous pastime to those in the business of handling and transporting ammunition.

Ship loads of ammunition were still arriving in the Philippines. This was ammo that had been put in the supply-pipeline months before in anticipation of the invasion of Japan. It wasn't just ammo. It was also guns, and trucks, and fuel, and tanks, and every other goddam thing that's needed to run a war. Apparently there was no way in which to stop that endless flow of materiel once it had been made and sent on its way. All of it was wasted. It's too bad that they didn't send the stuff to Chiang Kai-shek who was fighting the communists at that time. He could have used it.

Well anyway, the army was having a helluva time stockpiling all that stuff. It had so much ammunition that it started dumping its surplus in the bay. The Ts would bring in the new stuff and the army would take it off in trucks. Then the same trucks would return with "old" ammunition that was loaded aboard the Ts, taken out into the bay, and heaved over the side. It made quite a splash. The army supplied Filipino labor to do this work. This made the cargoes even more volatile.

In addition to the "old" American ammo, the army decided to "deep-six" all of the Jap ammo that it had in its possession. Apparently they didn't believe in burying any ammunition. Why should they go to so much trouble when the bay was there, and the Ts were there, and there was an endless supply of cheap labor to put to work. So the army loaded the Ts with mountains of ammo which they then had the job of dumping.   The American stuff was tricky enough to handle, but the Jap stuff was "dynamite."

LCT 170 was obliterated one rainy afternoon when it attempted to dispose of a cargo of Japanese explosives.   There were twelve sailors and twenty stevedores sitting atop that floating depot when it blew up.   The explosion left a mushroom cloud above it to mark the 170's last delivery site.   It was fortunate that the blast wave did not set off "sympathetic" explosions in all of the other ammo in the area.   That would have been a chain reaction to warm the heart of even a nuclear scientist. However, the sailors and merchant seamen in the area were not amused.   The Navy refused to handle any more Jap ammo after that.   But the Ts still had to dispose of the American stuff.

The only beneficial result of that tragic experience was that drinking was henceforth and forever forbidden aboard all ships engaged in that potentially explosive activity.   Those days were over. Quino's business doubled over night.

The town of Batangas experienced a revival second only to the "day of liberation."   The pom-pom girls had to bring in reinforcements to help them handle the crush.   That explosion had reminded the men that they were still alive, and that there were worse things than being stuck in the rain in Batangas Province.

In addition to materiel, there were also thousands of men in the supply pipeline. The war in Europe had ended on 8 May 1945. Before the month was out they were loading GIs on to transports for shipment to the Philippines. MacArthur wanted all of the men that the army no longer needed in Europe. Those men thought that they were going home when they walked up those gangways. Instead, they went directly to the Panama Canal, and from there directly to Luzon. They weren't at all happy about it. In fact, they were close to mutiny during their long voyage.

One rainy night the 166 got the call to go alongside the USS Sanborn (APA-193) to offload troops. It would be difficult to imagine a more disconsolate group of human beings. Smyth couldn't understand the haste with which they were unloaded - at night - in the rain? What was the hurry? The captain of the Sanborn had decided long ago to disembark them at the first opportunity. So one dark, rainy night the soldiers found themselves climbing down cargo nets that put them on a wet tank deck. Then they were deposited on a wet, sandy beach; marched along a wet, muddy road, and finally bivouacked in a wet, muddy field north of town. Welcome to the Philippines, you sad bastards!

Lake Taal is located about ten miles north of Batangas.   The lake fills the crater of an active volcano.   The surface of the lake covers one hundred square miles.   The smoking cone of the volcano rises to a height of a hundred feet in the center of the lake.   It is a magnificent sight.   It is such a lovely place that it has always been popular with whomever happens to be occupying the country at whatever time.

Several large two-story haciendas graced the southern shoreline of the lake. Those buildings were generously stocked with beer, booze, and broads for the spiritual edification of whatever transients happened to be in the neighborhood. One such group of pilgrims consisted of Frisch, Dugan, and Johnson.

These three had managed to finagle a 24-hour pass out of their CO on the basis of their not having been allowed to go ashore at Subic Bay.   They figured that a liberty was owed them, and they wanted to go to Lake Taal.   Pacelli and Temple also wanted to go, but the ensign could not allow all of his seamen to go at the same time.   They flipped a coin to determine who would go.   The winners were soon on the road with their thumbs in the air in the traditional pose of wheel-less supplicants. It didn't take them long to hitch a ride on a jeep that was going their way.   There was a lot of traffic on the lake road.

"Yeah, I go there all the time," said the soldier who was driving the jeep. "It's a great place if the MPs don't raid it."

"Why would they raid it?" asked the ingenuous Dugan.

" 'cause it's off-limits, that's why," replied the soldier.

"Why's it off-limits?" asked the second of the three dwarfs.

"Where've you guys been?" asked the soldier. "Don't you <u>know</u> about Lake Taal?"

"No, not much."

"Well it's the wildest fuckin' place in the world, that's all. Everybody gets screwed, blewed, and tatooed in Taal. Yes, sir, there's nothin' there but whiskey and wild, wild women. That's why the MPs keep raidin' the place. The army has so much trouble there that it's thinkin' of givin' it back to the Japs.   You're the first sailors I've seen goin' there. Where ya been?"

"We just got back from Manila," boasted an inspired Frisch. "Taal can't be any wilder than <u>that</u> place!"

"Are you kiddin'? Manila's an old lady compared with Taal. The women there wear more campaign ribbons than we do. But you won't see no Good Conduct ribbons among 'em. No sir, they've

got more battle stars than MacArthur has bullshit.
And <u>that's</u> sayin' somethin'."

"Where's the best place to go?"

"Hell, there ain't no <u>particular</u> place to go.
They're all about the same. Just find a hacienda
that ain't too crowded and pile in. You'll have the
time of your life. I shit you not."

"Is it expensive?" asked the frugal Dugan.

"Regular prices. A buck for a can of beer.
Ten bucks for a pint of booze."

"What about the girls?" asked the lusty Frisch.

"What about them?"

"How much do they get?"

"They get whatever you've got left in the
morning. But you better be generous or they'll cut
your balls off."

"Sounds like I'm finally gonna see some
combat," said Johnson.

"You better believe it," replied the soldier.

The half-hour trip ended at the southern tip of
the lake. The three mendicants piled out of the
jeep. They hesitatingly approached the nearest
hacienda. The wooden building was very old and
very handsome.

"Do you still want to go in?" asked Dugan
apprehensively.

"Hell yes," replied the fearless Frisch. "We've
come <u>this</u> far. We'll have to go through with it now."

"Why?"

"Well how would it look if we was to go back now?"

"Okay, secure all loose change and let's go!"

"Mother of God, have mercy on us sinners . . . mumbled the doubtful Dugan as they plunged fearlessly forward.

The ground floor of the Hacienda Bonita was one huge room that could have accommodated a basketball tournament. There was a bar running the length of the back wall. One end of the room boasted a bandstand and a blaring juke box. Several GIs were dancing with "hostesses" to the tune of **In the Mood.** The other end of the room featured three pool tables. Two of them were being used for their intended purpose. The third was being used as a connubial couch by a GI and his girlfriend. Our three young adventurers headed for the bar. They ordered beer. The barmaid said,

"Hey, where you fellas from? We hardly never see any sailors here. Don't sailors like girls?" she laughed.

"We're from Batangas," Frisch replied. "This ain't the only place that's got girls. There's girls in Batangas, too, ya know!"

"Okay, okay," she said,"don't get hot. Only joking. You want figgy-figgy?"

"Where?" asked Dugan, "on the pool table?"

"No, not on pool table, you crazy bastard. We go my room. Okay?"

"We just got here, for Chris' sake. Do ya mind if we have a beer first?"

"Sure. Have all beer you want. You want whiskey?"

"Not yet."

"You want dance?" asked one of the three hostesses that had joined them at the bar.

"Sure," said Frisch and Dugan as they went to do their version of the Lindy. Johnson remained at the bar with his beer and his B-girl.

"You no dance?" she asked as she ran her fingers through his blond hair.

"Not when I'm sober," he replied.

"You buy me drink?"

"Sure, what'll it be?"

"Champagne cocktail."

"Like hell," replied the knowledgeable Johnson. "I'm not buyin' you any goddam ginger ale called champagne and payin' five bucks for it. You drink what I'm drinkin' or go climb a rope."

"Climb a rope? What the hell you talkin' about you crazy bastard! I no climb rope, but I pull your rope." With that she reached for Johnson's cock, gave it a yank, and ran off laughing hysterically. Johnson looked after her with a pained expression on his face.

"What's the matter, sailor boy?" laughed the barmaid. "You no like Juanita?"

Silence.

"Good. You stay 'way from her. She bad girl. She bite your cock. You want 'nother beer?"

"Yeah, sure."

"Where you from?" she asked after she had brought him another beer.

"Nebraska."

"No shit? We had 'nother sailor from Nebraska in here a little while ago."

"Yeah? What became of him?" Johnson asked as he looked around the room.

"I don't know. He was hangin' 'round here for a while. He could be any place. I don't keep track of him. What the fuck you think I am, his mother?" she laughed.

When Dugan and Frisch returned to the bar Johnson told them about the mysterious sailor from Nebraska. Frisch asked the barmaid,

"What did he look like?"

"He young like you guys, but dirty. Jesus did he stink. They threw him in the lake to clean him up. He damn near drown, but he smell better," she laughed.

"Sidney!" Frisch and Dugan exclaimed simultaneously.

"Who's Sidney?" asked Johnson.

"He's our long-lost shipmate," Frisch said sadly.

"He's been missing since VJ-Day."

"How come I never heard of him?"

"We never talked about him 'cause we hoped he'd never show up. But if he's here we've gotta take him back with us. It's our duty as shipmates."

"Yeah, I guess you're right," remarked Dugan.

Frisch asked the barmaid, "Where is this guy from Nebraska?"

"I don't know. Maybe he passed out upstairs. Go take a look if you want," she said indifferently.

Topside looked like an enormous flophouse. Three couples were doing the shag at one end of the room. They found Sidney asleep on a bare cot. He was wearing army fatigues, but his usual odor overpowered his disguise and revealed him to his shipmates. They shook his comatose form. It grunted. They shook him again. An eye opened. It recognized Dugan and Frisch. Sidney sat upright on the edge of his cot.

"Dugan! Frisch! Jesus it's good to see you again. Who's this?" he asked looking suspiciously at Johnson.

"This is a new shipmate, Sidney. His name's Johnson. He's from Nebraska, too. He's the one who found ya."

"Thanks, Johnson, you saved my ass. I thought you was an SP. They're lookin' for me all over the place," he confided. "But I'm too smart for 'em. I even got out of Santo Tomas!"

"What the hell were you doin' in <u>there</u>?"

"I don't know. I ended up there somehow. They put me in the dungeon. I was in the same cell block with General Yamashita! I was right across from him. I kept yellin' at him, callin' him a dirty yellow son of a bitch," he laughed hysterically. "They took me out of there and put me somewhere else. Then I escaped and came here. I've been here for a while. I don't know how long. They won't let me go. They took all my money. They threw me in the lake. I haven't eaten in a week. They took my shoes. Get me outta here, will ya?"

"Sure," said the compassionate Dugan. "Let's go."

When the four of them got to the bottom of the stairway they were met by the hostile manager of the hacienda.

"He don't go nowhere 'til he pay his bill!" said the manager as he attempted to grab Sidney.

"What bill?"

"He been here all week eating and drinking like king. You think this is for free?"

"He don't look like he's had too much to eat."

"He eat plenty, drink plenty, figgy-figgy alla time.   He pay up or he no leave!" he yelled as he attempted to grab the elusive Sidney again.

Several other male Filipinos had joined the group at the foot of the stairway. The sailors started to push their way through.   The Filipinos pushed back. When the GIs saw their countrymen in trouble they went to their aid on the double. Then more Filipinos went to the aid of their countrymen. Before our quartet knew what was happening they were in the middle of a Pier 6 brawl.   The MPs arrived. Our foursome barely escaped through a side door.   They   staggered down the road back to Batangas. A truck gave them a lift to the port. The old reliable 166 was waiting for them on the beach. They all fell onto their bunks and went to sleep. It began to rain again.

The next morning they gave Sidney a good breakfast and a brand new set of shiny khakis. They threw his fatigues into Temple's ragbag.   Ensign Smyth did not press charges against Sidney for being AWOL. If only half of what he said was true, then he had been punished enough for his transgressions.

They never went back to Lake Taal again.

Chapter 14

Auld Lang Syne

"What the hell is that goddam riot all about?" yelled Ensign Smyth from his rack to no one in particular.

"It's the bosun," replied the cook. "He's chasin' the monkey."

"Why?" asked the ensign as he slowly sat up on the edge of his rack. His powers of comprehension were somewhat under a cloud that morning. In fact, his powers were usually under a cloud in the morning. He looked about him for his pack of Luckies.

The cook replied, "Because it tore all the labels off the cans we stacked on the shelves yesterday. Now I can't tell the peaches from the string beans."

The ensign painfully stood up, wrapped a towel around his mid-section, and stepped unsteadily through the hatch and onto the tank deck. There he stood as though transfixed as he watched the bosun catch the monkey by its leash, swing the bewildered creature around his head three times, and then let it sail for a cable's length before plunging into hungry waters of Batangas Bay. It was all over before the benumbed ensign could act to prevent that most singular event.

"There, you little bastard!" yelled the bosun as

he shook his fist at an ever-widening circle on the surface of the bay. "And if I ever see the likes of you again, I'll cut ya goddam tail off and ram it down ya goddam throat!" Then he turned to confront his commanding officer with, "And that's the last goddam animal I ever want to see on this goddam ship!"

Ensign Smyth had nothing to say in response to this declaration which apparently was to be the final word on the subject of pets aboard the 166. He shrugged his shoulders. Then he returned to his rack to resume his slumbers. The ensign knew better than to get into a hassle with Bosun Jazinski when he had his Polish up.

After disposing of the monkey, the bosun went looking for Sidney, who luckily for him, was still on the beach after an all-night liberty. The monkey had come aboard with Sidney late one sultry night when the bosun was asleep. When the monkey made its debut the next morning the crew was taken with the novelty of having such a creature aboard. Not many ships in the USN have such a pet. They were soon to learn why.

Sidney rigged a line forward of the leading edge of the tarpaulin. To this line was attached a leash of about ten feet in length, the bitter end of which was secured about the monkey's waist.

Thus the creature was given a large area in which to cavort, and the crew was given a diversion that was sorely needed. The scene was thus set for the great monkey trial.

What do monkey's eat? Why bananas of course. So Sidney got a bunch of them from a passing vendor. The monkey did enjoy them. And he did enjoy throwing their skins all over the tank deck. And he enjoyed "dumping' all over the area after he had eaten the bananas!

Now it must be understood that there are certain things that <u>are</u> <u>not</u> <u>done</u> in the US Navy, but the monkey did not know this. However, the bosun knew these things all too well. It is to his credit that he did not explode the <u>first</u> time that he witnessed the desecration of his deck. His solution to this aberration was to assign Sidney to the simian-sanitation detail. Sidney was the likely choice since it was he who had brought the creature aboard in the first place; and in the second place, he also had certain simian characteristics.

Monkeys are by nature very curious and very destructive. Everything that the creature could reach was either eaten, or torn up, or tossed asunder. The tank deck soon presented an unbelievable mess. The bosun became surly. The crew became fascinated. Bets were laid. Who would get it first - Sidney or the monkey?

The monkey was blissfully unaware of all of this. He must have been or else he would have changed his habits. But no, he went right on with his suicidal lifestyle, unmindful of the change for the worse in the bosun's disposition.

The climax of all of this came one day when a boat tied alongside with a load of canned goods for the galley. The cases were muscled aboard and were stacked within proximity of the monkey. The creature eyed all of this very coolly. He didn't make a move until that night when he was left to his own devices. And devious devices they were, too. For that very night he opened every case and tore the labels from every can that had a label on it.

The crew first became aware of this turn of events when they heard the bosun roaring and swearing and crying as he chased the monkey through the debris. The rest you already know.

Sidney barely escaped a similar fate. Instead, he was given the job of cleaning up the mess and of attempting to put the labels back on the cans in their proper affiliation. Every time that the cook opened a can of "corn" only to find spinach instead, Sidney was given another cursing and all of the spinach that he could eat. From then on when he went ashore, he drank in moderation, steered clear of the bosun, and returned to the ark unencumbered by animals of any description.

The following news items were extracted from the 2 December 1945 issue of the **Navy News.** These items were read aloud by Essex one night to a few

shipmates who happened to be lounging in the compartment of the 166.

"San Francisco (UP) A log jam of servicemen returned from the Pacific and awaiting transportation from the San Francisco Bay area apparently was breaking up with scores of railroad passenger cars arriving here.

"Twenty-one trainloads carrying more than 10,000 servicemen were dispatched here in the last two days. It is estimated that the movement of at least two trains a day could be maintained. About 1,200 men were reported moving east by air."

"Ain't that nice," said the cook.

"Here's another one," said Essex.

"Tokyo (UP) Approximately one-third of the US servicemen who were in the Pacific Ocean areas on VJ-Day have been sent back to the US, Navy sources disclosed."

"Well they ain't sent one-third of us back to the States," yelled the bosun.

"Wait a minute," said Essex. "Here's some good news."

"Washington (AP) Brewers will be permitted to make about 20percent more beer and ale during the December-February period than was previously indi- cated."

"That's so all of them returned heroes will have enough suds to see them through the holiday season," said the cook, "otherwise they might get violent."

(The following item was printed on the back page of that issue of the **Navy News.** It evoked no interest at that time and place:

Alhambra, Calif. (UP) LTCMDR Richard Nixon of Whittier was chosen as the Republican candidate to oppose Jerry Voorhis for the 12th district's Congressional seat.)

"I can't believe that I'm gonna spend one more Christmas on this goddam bucket!" yelled the bosun. "It ain't fair! I was the first one over here, and now I'm gonna be the last one home!Ain't I ever gonna get off this goddam thing!"

"Sure we will," interjected the ensign as he stepped into the mess area in a desperate attempt to prevent the bosun from doing something rash. "I promise you that we'll all be off this bucket by the end of the year! How's that?"

"Are you sure?"

"Sure I'm sure. I got the inside scoop last night in the OC. This whole group is scheduled to be turned over to the government of the Philippines. We've only got four, maybe five, weeks to wait. Then it's goodbye Batangas!"

"No shit?"

"I shit you not."

"Hooray!" yelled the bosun as he embraced Smyth. "This calls for a celebration. Let's go to Quino's. I'm buyin!"

So with that ringing in their ears, they went into the night in pursuit of the golden lager.   In reality, it was not a pursuit since they took their lager with them.   They had a unique arrangement with the publican -   the sailors would bring cases of beer to him. He would buy them for ten dollars a case; then he would put them in his "reefer" for cooling, then he would sell the beer back to them for one dollar a can.   It was crazy economics, but it worked.

The celebration continued into the wee hours. Eventually they all piled out of Quino's after he had threatened them with a samurai sword.   Then he led them   back   to   the   beach   in   the   manner   of   the pie-eyed piper   of Batangas. He left them on the beach where they dropped. The 166 was not there!

Ensign Smyth, in his wisdom, had withdrawn the ship at midnight because he knew the condition that his men would be in if they did not return by 2400.   The 166 was tantalyzingly anchored about 100 yards off the beach.

The men protested this singular act for a moment, and then they surrendered to the beer, the embracing blackness, and the warm sand. Soon they were all asleep except for two - Sidney and Johnson.

"I'll race you out to the ship," Sidney challenged Johnson.

"For how much?" asked Johnson.

"This farm boy has twenty bucks that says he can beat you."

"Are you kiddin"? You don't have twenty pesos!"

"Oh yeah! I got money on the ship. Plenty money. Whatsamatter Johnson, ya chicken?"

"All right, you cornhuskin' sonofabitch, let's go."

The water was surprisingly warm and phosphorescent. It took them a long time to get out to the T. Then they couldn't figure out a way to get aboard her. They swam around her rusty sides until they found the short ladder next to the anchor guard. Johnson went up first. When he turned around to give Sidney a hand, he was gone! However, there was a great swirl of phosphoresence to be seen not far below the surface. Sidney came up once, screamed, and then was seen no more. Johnson went berserk. He was about to jump into the water when Frankie grabbed him from behind and held on to him. The uproar brought Smyth out of his cabin. The two of them wrestled Johnson to the deck. Then the fight went out of him, and the sobbing began. Frankie stayed with him.

Smyth turned on all topside lights. Then he

turned on the anchor winch.   Once he heard the anchor banging on the stern he started the engines and headed for the beach.   By then all of the men were running around yelling   questions.   The 166 swooshed softly onto the shore.   Smyth secured the engines and then ran forward to lower the ramp. But first he made sure that no one was standing where it would fall.   One tragedy per night was quite enough.

Johnson by then was hanging over the port side chains heaving his guts.   He was shaking violently.   Frankie was still with him.

After Smyth had finished trying to explain things to the men, Frankie spoke up,"Is 'tiburon', shark.   Is bad at night.   I should have warned you, but I never knew you'd swim at night.   You never swim.   I sorry."

"It's not   your   fault, Frankie," said the ensign, "it's mine for letting these maniacs run wild. Well I've had it!   From now on you will be back here by 2400 or by God I'll have your ass   thrown in the brig for being A-WOL! And anyone who comes back too drunk for duty will be busted!   Is that clear? Good. Dismissed!"

The   men hadn't heard that command since they left bootcamp, but they still knew what it meant.   They quietly went to their   respective bunks and cots.   Smyth went to stand by Johnson.   He had recovered from his attack of the heaves, but he still had the shakes. Frankie and the ensign sat with him for a while on the wheel-house deck. Then the three of them went below to their bunks and cots. Smyth was the last one to fall asleep.

Everyone slept -in the next day. But Frankie, as usual, was the first one up. He climbed to the wheel-house deck, as was his morning habit, in order to hang his ass over the stern so that he could relieve himself. While in that position he happened to glance to his left where the anchor was secured. Straddling one anchor-fluke was the lower half of Sidney's torso. Frankie emptied himself expeditiously. He stood up, pulled up his pants, jumped to the tank deck, ran into Smyth's cabin, shook him and whispered, "Wake up, sir. Is something terrible! Oh madre di dios, what are we going to do with it?"

"Do with what?" asked the completely beat ensign.

"Come, I show you."

Smyth slowly eased himself out of his bunk, put on some clothes, and followed Frankie up to the wheel-house deck. Frankie pointed it out to the ensign who promptly heaved on the remains of Seaman "Sidney" Mack. "Get the bosun," he gasped.

The bosun had seen such things before. He was very professional in his solution to the problem. First he thrust a boat hook under the belt that was still secured to the dungarees that still remained on

Sidney's lower half. Then he pulled the remains off of the anchor fluke and dropped them into the water with the boat hook still secured to the belt. The bosun held on to the boat hook while Frankie and the ensign launched the boat. The remains were hauled into the boat, the boat was pulled up on the beach, the cargo was covered with a tarp. Then the bosun hitch-hiked into town to the Army's Graves Registration Office. They returned to the 166 in a truck to claim what was left of Sidney. They put the remains in a box and drove away with it. Sidney was buried the next day in the military cemetery.

The day before Christmas 1945 Ensign Smyth put the 166 alongside a Navy supply ship that had somehow blundered into the bay. It was the first such vessel that they had seen since Leyte Gulf. Ensign Smyth went aboard, presented his compliments to the Officer-of-the-Deck, and then requested rations for a crew of fifteen even though there were only eight enlisted men left in his ship's company. The presumptuous ensign's request was granted! He was issued a case of chickens, a wheel of cheese, a case of apples, ten cases of beer, a case of cigarettes, sacks of flour, rice, and coffee beans; cases of canned fruit and vegetables, and a very large turkey! The whole order was placed in one cargo net and was carefully lowered onto the deck of the 166. The grateful crew carried their gifts into the compartment for sorting, storage, and consumption. The case of apples was the first item to be consumed.

On Christmas Day the crew stayed in the compartment to drink beer and to watch Evers prepare the turkey. Frankie was also busy baking special Filipino goodies. A family atmosphere prevailed, for indeed they <u>were</u> a family whose time together was growing short. They would soon be scattered to the winds, but they would never forget one another, nor their last Christmas together, till the day they died.

The week after Christmas was marked by one more hassle with the army. It seemed that the military authorities were beginning to suspect that there might be a leak in their pipeline. They determined to plug the leak by assigning Filipino soldiers to stand guard over the cargoes while the Ts were on the beach waiting to be unloaded. This didn't bother the crewmen because they had already taken what they needed before the T hit the beach. But the presence of the soldiers was an irritant to a certain degree. After all, they did cast an aspersion on the integrity of their group!

One morning one of the guards approached the lowered ramp of the 166. Pacelli was up forward at that moment doing something of little importance. The guard requested permission to come aboard (this being standard procedure). Pacelli responded:

"Sure, come ahead, knock yourself out if you want."

Now this harmless remark, which was in common usage at that time, was mis-interpreted by the Filipino as being a threat. He thought that Pacelli was threatening to knock him out! He fled the scene, reported the outrage to his sergeant, and then all hell broke loose.

A truck load of armed MPs suddenly materialized on the sand iin front of the ramp. They came charging aboard without so much as a by-your-leave. They arrested Evers, Frisch, Temple, Johnson, and the maleloquent Seaman Pacelli. The others were in town at that moment getting squared away on their transfer papers and the transfer of the 166. When they returned to their T they were informed by Frankie about the incarceration of the unlucky quintet.

"Those goddam bastards!" yelled the ensign in reference to the army in general. "They've always hated our guts. Now they think they've got the right to stick it to us, do they? Well they've got another think coming!"

With that exclamation ringing in their ears they walked down the beach to the 182 and LT Jameson. The lieutenant was just as outraged as the ensign. The two of them piled into the lieutenant's jeep. They drove off to visit with the Provost

Martial's office in town.   The PM that day was a certain Colonel Anderson.   He had a familiar look about him.

"Ah yes," said the colonel after he had listened to the two outraged junior officers. "I remember LCT 166 very well. I believe that it was down in Hollandia that I first became aware of that pirate ship. I don't remember either of you gentlemen, but I do re-call a red- faced officer in a white bathrobe. I believe that his name was Brower, or something like that. As you see, gentlemen,I have a remarkable memory. I have an especially painful memory of a case of scotch that was stolen from me by those same rogues presently languishing in my stockade where they will remain for <u>twenty</u> <u>fucking</u> <u>years</u> if I do not get my scotch back!"

"Colonel," said Smyth, "we don't know what you're talking about. We had nothing to do with the disappearance of your scotch. But if it will take a case of scotch to get our men out of here, then we will get you a case of scotch. Any particular brand?"

"Yes, of course, but you won't be able to get it in this godforsaken place.   <u>Any</u> scotch will do under <u>these</u> circumstances.   In the meantime I will introduce your men to some discipline which will, I am sure, be a novel experience for them."

"Yes, sir, Colonel," said Smyth, "but don't lean too hard on them or they might get violent. They're all a little 'asiatic'. If they were crazy enough to steal your scotch, as you say, imagine what shape they're in <u>now</u>! I won't be responsible for their actions if you provoke them."

"Get out of here!" yelled the colonel. "And don't come back without my scotch. You're <u>all</u> nuts if you ask me!"

Once the two junior officers were back in the jeep, Jameson asked, "So what'll we do now?"

"We'll go see Quino. He must have some scotch. He's got everything else."

Quino <u>did</u> have a case of scotch, but the price was high - a truck load of beer.

"Can you get a truck?" Smyth asked Quino.

"Sure, I can get <u>anything</u>."

"Then get down to the 166 pronto before the army gets there, and help yourself to all of the beer we've got. You explain to Frankie. Hurry."

Quino ran outside and started yelling at a dozen people in Tagalog. A truck soon materialized. A gang jumped aboard. Immediately they were tearing down the road to the port. An hour later they were back with their haul of purloined potables. Quino gave the two naval officers a case of scotch - good stuff, too. They put the case in their jeep. Then they returned to the colonel's prefecture.

"Well I'll be damned," he said when he saw the scotch. It's amazing. Such resourcefulness. Would you gentlemen like a drink?"

"No thank you, Colonel. We just want to get our men back to the ship so that we can bring in more supplies for you, sir."

"Now that's the attitude to have, Ensign. By God there's hope for you people yet. All right, Sergeant, bring those naval personnel in here. And don't provoke them along the way," he laughed.

The five angry POWs filed into the room. The ensign gave them a look that told them to keep their mouths shut. The colonel spoke,

"You men have been released thanks to the ingenuity of your officers and the generosity of the United States Army. I hope that in the future you will refrain from threatening any of my men in any way whatsoever, or by God I'll keep you here for twenty fucking years! Is that clear?"

"Yes, sir," they mumbled.

"All right. Get them out of here, gentlemen. And keep them out of here, or the next time they won't be so lucky."

They didn't wait for any more ceremony. They all piled out into the street and headed for the beach. The officers went by jeep. The yard-birds went the hard way - on foot. But at least they didn't have to do any hard time.

As Smyth drove Jameson back to the port he said, "Well that was easy enough. I didn't think we'd get them back that fast."

"The colonel didn't have a legal leg to stand on," Jameson said, "and he knew it. The army has no jurisdiction over naval personnel when they're not ashore. The army's not even allowed to come on board without our permission. Didn't you know that?"

"Then why didn't you say something instead of making me go through all that business with the scotch."

"Because that was the easy way. If we had gone the legal route we'd still be back there, and your men might have had to spend a month in the stockade. I knew you didn't want that, so I kept my mouth shut. But if he'd gotten cute after getting his scotch, then I would have thrown the book at him. When everything else fails, try the law."

"Are you a lawyer or something?"

"No, but I hope to be. I'm going to law school when I get home. God but that sounds good - when I get home, not if I get home."

"Yeah. We should get our orders any day now. That means back to Subic Bay. Will we get there the same way as before?"

"Yes, only this time we'll go in five Ts. The rest of them will remain here for the use of the Filipinos. They're going to use them for ferries."

"Well isn't that what <u>we've</u> been using them for?" asked Smyth. "Inter-island ferries?"

"Yes, I guess you're right. But from now on they'll be ferrying strange peacetime cargoes. The old war horses . . ."

" . . . mules . . ."

" . . . are being retired to an exotic sea pasture."

"I'll miss them," said Smyth. "They've played an unforgettable part in my life. And I'll miss the men. We've shared a comradeship which I shall probably never experience again."

"My God, you sound almost sentimental!"

"I read somewhere that it's not unusual for seamen to get sentimental about their ships and their shipmates, but that they never get sentimental about the sea. Isn't that extraordinary?" asked the ensign.

"Not at all. Only people who have never spent a lot of time at sea are sentimental about it. The sea is a deadly bitch who will kill you the first chance she gets. Every seaman knows that. I'm not sentimental about her, but I sure respect her. I just hope that she lets us go."

"My God, you sound almost superstitious," mocked the ensign.

"A little healthy superstition never hurt anyone. It's especially beneficial to those who go down to the sea in ships."

"And don't forget 'those in peril on the sea'," laughed Smyth.

"For God's sake, don't laugh! She may hear you. We're too close to going home to taunt her now."

"You're really serious, aren't you?" said Smyth.

"You're damn right I'm serious. Haven't you ever heard of the **Ancient Mariner** or the **Flying Dutchman**?"

"<u>They</u> were not written by seamen."

"No, but they originated in the <u>minds</u> of seamen."

"So did **Moby Dick, Two Years Before the Mast,** and **The Long Voyage Home**," said the literate Mister Smyth.

"Right. <u>Those</u> are the books to read if you want to get the truth about the sea and ships and seamen. Books written by seamen who <u>sailed</u> as seamen down in the foc'sle, before the mast."

"Abaft the beam. Athwart the deck. Atop the yard. A slip of the lip . . ."

" . . . may sink a ship."

"Ya know," laughed the ensign. "I think we're getting out of here just in time."

"No, you're wrong. We should have gotten out of here long ago. Now it's too late. We're asiatic."

"You mean crazy?"

"No, I mean 'asiatic' which is a temporary mental aberration brought on by eating too much fried chicken.   But don't worry, its symptoms will gradually fade as we gradually approach the Golden Gate of the Golden State."

"On a golden plate," added Smyth.

"Please, don't start that again," he laughed.

"Well thanks for the ride, the help, and the laughs," said Smyth as the jeep stopped in front of his 166.   "We'll have to get together again some time under more pleasant circumstances."

"Yeah, like under a palm tree at Olongapo with a case of suds and a brace of girls."

"Now you're talkin'.   Keep thinking positive thoughts like that and soon your eccentric behavior will become less and less obtrusive. Then you may be allowed to re-enter the main stream of American life.   You may even be allowed to practice law. Just don't practice on me!"

"Smyth, you're a jewel.   Truly a diamond in the rough.   It's a pity that we didn't get together sooner.   It would have moved the time along more swiftly and more pleasantly.   Well maybe we'll be able to spend more time together in the near future."

"Yes, I'd like that," responded Smyth.   "And I may need a good lawyer some day."

"Yes, I'm sure you will," laughed Jameson. "In fact, I might even say that it's inevitable."

"Well no one ever said that it was easy to be eccentric."

"Quite right," laughed the lieutenant as he drove down the beach to his 181. "See you later."

But the ensign did not get to see LT Jameson later because he was killed in a jeep accident the next day. The sea was kinder to him than that.

Their last week in Batangas was marked by a plane crash, the theft of a tank, and the discovery of a new way of catching fish.

The fish-catching idea came to Pacelli one afternoon while he was watching a work-gang drop cases of hand grenades over the side into the deep. He surreptitiously put one case aside for his personal use. When the tank deck was completely cleared of all ammunition, Pacelli opened his case of grenades. He took one out, pulled its pin, and dropped it over the side. From far below came a muffled "plonk" that was a great disappointment to him. He expected more of a depth-charge type of reaction. He decided not to waste any more grenades in those deep waters. Another plan was forming in his mind.

The road that ran parallel to the beach separated the sandy area from acres and acres of rice paddies. Pacelli knew that the farmers put fish in their shallow paddies for some bucolic reason. Pacelli decided to test his new idea for catching fish the easy way. So one day he and Evers found themselves standing on the in-board side of the road throwing hand grenades far into the paddies. When they had exhausted their supply they waded into the muck to observe the results of their experiment. The results were spectacular. They soon collected a basket full of fish. They also collected a great deal of attention from everyone including the farmer who owned the paddies. He came after them swinging a big bolo. Our two fishermen took one look at him, dropped the basket, and took off for the 166. The farmer chased them as far as the basket. He picked it up and smiled. Thus mollified he did not further pursue the piscatorial Pacelli and his brandy-brained buddy. Thus did the famous fishing experiement end. However, that was not the end of the vexations suffered by that farmer, for the very next day a DC-3 made an emergency landing on his paddies. The pilot made a beautiful landing. Mud and rice and fish and feces flew through the air for a hundred feet in all directions. It was a memorable sight. The pilot sloshed away from the wreck. The farmer grew despondent. He gave up trying to grow rice in that area. He applied for relief through the US Dept. of Ag's Extension Service. He was the first native of Batangas to receive welfare. They recently erected a monument to him in the town square.

The great tank robbery occurred one hot afternoon when Essex and the bosun were in a mischievous mood and there were four behemoths squatting on their deck. They climbed aboard one of the lead tanks, opened its hatch, and dropped out of sight. The next thing they knew they had the damn thing started! It slowly rumbled over the ramp, up the beach, across the road, into the rice paddies, and back onto the road. They got as far as the middle of town before they were stopped by another tank that was parked athwart the road. They were hauled before Colonel Anderson. He couldn't believe it. The two men spent the night in the colonel's stockade, but they were released in the morning because the Ts were leaving that day for Subic Bay. The colonel did not want to do <u>anything</u> that might delay their departure, so he released Essex and the bosun without further ado. He even gave them a "God speed" as they left his office. Their walk back to the beach was a triumphal march. Quino even gave them free beers as they passed his place. It was their final and finest hour in Batangas.

Ensign Smyth was promoted to LTJG Smyth. He was put in charge of the convoy because he was the only officer left with such experience. To celebrate <u>his</u> promotion he in turn promoted every member of his crew one jump. Hank Johnson had a choice of ratings. He could either be a Gunner's

Mate Third Class, or he could be a Boatswain's Mate Third Class. He chose the latter out of respect for Chief Boatswain's Mate Jazinski.

Each T was crowded with a double crew, so Smyth decided to make it a straight shot for Subic Bay with no side trips or layovers. The Ts that were left on the beach at Batangas were stripped of everything that could be eaten or drunk. The men swore that by the time they got to Subic there would not be a thing left that could be digested. Thus their wakes were marked by hundreds of floating empties, cases, and cartons. They were faithful to their oath.

After an un-eventful 24-hour journey the 166 dropped her hook in the mud of the Subic anchorage. The other four Ts tied on to her. Several LCVPs came out to carry the men and their gear ashore. And thus the Ts were left empty and quiet to swing forlornly in the restless tides; rusty reminders of a once great amphibious force in which they had played a significant, unruly, and relatively unknown role. I shit you not.

* * *